Being
Danny's
Dog

Books By Phyllis Reynolds Naylor

Being Danny's Dog

PHYLLIS REYNOLDS NAYLOR

ATHENEUM BOOKS FOR YOUNG READERS

Atheneum Books for Young Readers
An imprint of Simon & Schuster Children's Publishing Division
1230 Avenue of the Americas
New York, New York 10020

Text copyright © 1995 by Phyllis Reynolds Naylor

Book design by Michael Nelson
The text of this book is set in Goudy Old Style

First edition
Printed in the United States of America
10 9 8 7 6 5 4 3 2 1

Library of Congress Cataloging-in-Publication Data

Naylor, Phyllis Reynolds.
Being Danny's dog / by Phyllis Reynolds Naylor. — 1st ed.
p.   cm.
Summary: Ten-year-old T.R. and his twelve-year-old brother Danny move to
Rosemary Acres with their mother and find new friends as well as a lot of community
rules to follow.
ISBN 0-689-31756-5
[1. Brothers—Fiction.   2. Moving, Household—Fiction.
3. Divorce—Fiction.   4. Responsibility—Fiction.
5. Friendship—Fiction.]   I. Title.
PZ7.N24Bf   1995   [Fic]—dc20   95-5280   CIP   AC

Reprinted by arrangement with Atheneum Books for Young Readers,
Simon & Schuster Children's Publishing Division.

To John, who did the door

Contents

Cajun Drive

I knew I was Danny's dog when he gave me a Chicago Bears cap for my birthday—not a new one that you could buy in any drugstore, but his own, autographed by the quarterback.

Mom gave me some jeans, Dad sent a camera, but Danny gave me what he treasured most. Like a loyal sheepdog, I'd do anything for Danny.

After I'd unwrapped it, though, I started to worry because I'd heard that when a person is thinking about suicide, he gives away his possessions, so I just asked Danny right out.

"I've hardly started to live yet," he said. "Why would I think about dying?"

For the last two years we'd lived in an apartment at Aunt Celia's—Aunt Cis we call her. Then Mom got this big bunch of money in the divorce settlement and decided it was time for a new start. She doesn't teach in the city, for one thing, and wanted to be closer to her job. If we lived in Chicago any longer, she said, we'd be stunted by carbon monoxide. She wanted us to live close enough to the city that we could drive in to the museums now and then, but far enough out that we knew what clover smelled like.

"I already know what clover smells like," I told her.

"But I want you to smell it every day," said Mom.

So after summer vacation began, we rode out to look at townhouses in a new development called Rosemary Acres.

Danny and I didn't want to go. We liked it at Aunt Celia's, and didn't care that there wasn't any grass in the backyard. All the way to Rosemary Acres we sat in the backseat and did our best to look crabby. When Danny wants to look crabby, he gets this little frown right between his eyes, and sort of puffs out his lips. I leaned back in the seat and frowned, but when I tried to stick out my lips, I blew a spit bubble.

Mom was watching through the rearview mirror. She had on these sunglasses that were darker at the top than at the bottom, but I could tell by the way she tipped her head that she was looking at us.

"It's a beautiful place," she said. "It opened only five months ago. The builder named it after his wife."

"I'll bet she was big as a horse," said Danny. "Acres and acres of Rosemary."

I laughed. Mom didn't.

I'll admit there were more trees the farther we got from Chicago, and it wasn't as noisy or as hot. We even passed a farm with a silo and everything, but when we got to Rosemary Acres, it looked as though the builder had bulldozed the whole place before he put up his houses. It was like a desert almost.

Mom drove us around before we went to the sales office. Everything looked new—the sidewalks, the lamp-posts, even the little trees, which were so skinny they had to be held up with sticks and wires.

"Basil Boulevard," Mom said aloud, as we slowly turned a corner. And then, farther on, "Pepper Road." She laughed.

I stared out the window, watching for the next street sign. Cinnamon Court, it read. All the streets were named after spices. I looked at Danny. He pretended to vomit.

There was a playground for little kids at Sage Circle, but nobody was there, and a man-made lake to one side of the development, with only one duck that they proba-bly got from a pet shop. We saw a few people getting in and out of cars, but that was all.

"Mom, they all look like yuppies! There aren't any guys my age!" Danny protested.

"Well, now, how do you know that?" Mom said. She turned at the next street, Curry Lane, and down at the end, where the road stopped, we saw a tall, thin boy, maybe a little older than Danny, shooting baskets.

"Look!" said Mom, as though she'd just sighted land, and pulled right up to him.

"No, Mom!" Danny whispered, sinking down in the seat. But Mom already had her head out the window.

"Excuse me," she called.

The boy looked at her, shot another basket, then wiped his forehead on his T-shirt and came over. He glanced at us in the backseat.

"Yeah?"

"We're trying to find the office," Mom said. "I made a few too many turns."

"Turn left onto Basil." The boy motioned with the ball. "Go all the way down to Fennel. It's there on the corner."

Mom smiled. One thing about Mom, she has a really nice smile, with a dimple in one cheek. "Thank you," she said. "Do you live here?"

The boy nodded and studied Danny and me again. "Couple houses back."

"Do you find enough to do here? Are there other people your age?" Mom should have been a census taker.

The boy shrugged. "Enough, I guess," he said, and then turned his back and shot another basket.

"Mom, for Pete's sake, move on!" Danny breathed. So Mom turned the car around and headed for Basil.

"These are the only two units left," Miss Quinn, the resident manager, told us. She was a young, thin woman in high heels, and we followed her up the stairs. The thing about townhouses is that they sure have a lot of stairs.

"How many in your family, Mrs. . . . ?" Miss Quinn glanced at us over her shoulder.

"Scarlino," said Mom. "It's Italian." She always adds that, even though it's Dad's name and she's Irish. Mom's big on knowing your roots. "There are just the three of us."

She's big on roots, but she's not so big on Dad. I asked her once why they'd named me T.R.—initials instead of a name—and she said it's so I can choose my own name when I grow up. Then she laughed and said they'd named me after Theodore Roosevelt. But Grandma Flora told me I'd really been named after my dad— Thomas Richard—and if I wanted, I could call myself Thomas Richard, Jr. I didn't want to.

"Well, Mrs. Scarlino, there are three bedrooms up here, so you could each have one for yourself," Miss Quinn said when we reached the top. There was a business-like smile on her face whenever she was talking to Mom, but it disappeared when she wasn't. It disappeared especially when Danny or I put our hands on the walls.

"I get this one," I said, sticking my head in a room that had blue and yellow racing cars on the wallpaper.

"So what?" Danny went into the second bedroom and pointed to the window. "Look."

"What?"

"It faces the house over there."

"So?"

"So if there was a woman taking off her clothes, I could turn out my lights and watch."

If I was twelve instead of ten, I would have thought of that.

We went back down to see the lower levels.

"It's really nice," Mom said. "A fireplace and everything. But I want to see the other unit, too."

We got in Miss Quinn's car again and drove to the second townhouse. I looked for a bedroom that faced somebody's window, but there wasn't one.

"It's lovely," said Mom, "but there's no fireplace."

"That's right. The houses on Parsley Place have them, but these don't," Miss Quinn told her.

Parsley Place? I looked at Danny.

"The other street's Parsley Place?" he asked Miss Quinn after Mom had gone into the dining room. She nodded.

I was fooling around with the built-in microwave, and Danny came over. "I'm not going to live there," he whispered to me. "Can you imagine telling anyone you live on *Parsley* Place? Jeez!" And then he asked Miss Quinn, "What street is this house on?"

"Cajun Drive," she said.

Cajun Drive, yeah! I looked at Danny and grinned. He smiled a little, too.

When Mom came back in the kitchen, we told her we liked this house best.

"Really?" She seemed surprised.

"Yeah. It's got a bigger yard," Danny said.

"But it hasn't got a fireplace!"

"The stove's nicer," I said.

"The stoves are exactly the same!" Mom told me.

"One advantage of this unit, Mrs. Scarlino, is that there's a mud room off the kitchen," said Miss Quinn.

"Yeah, Mom!" I said. *What the heck was a mud room?*

"Just what I always wanted!" said Danny.

Mom couldn't seem to decide.

"Well, if we're going to move, I want to live in this house," Danny said.

"Me too," I put in.

"I don't want to rush you, Mrs. Scarlino, but I do have a couple coming at four to see this house," Miss Quinn said. "End units are very popular, you know."

Mom looked from me to Danny and back again. "It *does* have a side yard . . . and cross ventilation. That yard might be pretty important to you guys . . . ." Suddenly she reached for her checkbook and took a deep breath. "I'll take it," she said.

It was only when we were in the car going home that we told Mom why we liked the second one best. We wished we hadn't. She pulled right off the road and turned around in the seat.

"You mean the only reason you chose that house was the name of the *street?*" she said. "I just put a deposit on a townhouse because of the *street?*"

I couldn't see her eyes behind her glasses, but she was really upset. I hated myself. But Danny saved us. Danny always comes through.

"Joke, joke!" he said. "It's a great house, Mom. We can play touch football in the side yard."

"Yeah, and I like the bathroom better," I said.

Mom sighed, then turned around, and edged slowly back into traffic.

"For your information," she told us, "'Cajun' is not even a spice. It's the name of an ethnic group, and also refers to a style of cooking. Cajun Drive is the one street in the whole development that is named incorrectly." (Mom's a teacher.)

"I still like it," I said.

Danny and I didn't dare look at each other. We sat like rocks all the way home. We'd given up a fireplace, a room with racing cars on the walls, and a window where you could watch naked ladies, just so we wouldn't have to live on Parsley Place.

As we were getting out of the car, I asked Danny, "What if she pulled down her blinds?"

"Who?"

"The lady you were going to watch out of your window. What would you do then?"

"Oh, her," said Danny. He shrugged. "I don't know. Find something else to do, I guess."

A Little
Something
from Dad

The night before we moved, Aunt Cis gave us a party. Celia is Dad's sister, but Mom's actually closer to her than she is to her own sister, Mavis. Aunt Mavis came to the party, though, with her husband, Lyle. Keith, who is Mom and Mavis's brother, was invited, too. The only person missing was Dad, but if he'd been there, we wouldn't be moving at all. We'd probably still live in that same house we used to rent near the university.

"So you finally got yourselves a yard!" Keith said.

I started to say that Danny and I liked streets and sidewalks just fine, but I could see Mom watching, so I said, "Yeah, we've got big plans for that yard." Mom looked pleased.

We ate Aunt Celia's famous pepper steak, filled up on bread and salad and all the pop we could drink. Then everybody set to work helping us finish the packing. Half our furniture had been in storage for two years, and I wondered what it would be like to sleep in my own bed.

"Truthfully, Danny, are you ever going to wear this again?" Aunt Cis asked, holding up a T-shirt with the sleeves cut out.

"All the time," said Danny, and put it in his bag. I'd tried cutting the sleeves off one of my T-shirts, too, but I'd cut a big gash in Mom's tablecloth while I was at it, and she'd thrown out my T-shirt along with the tablecloth.

Aunt Cis went on sorting, and talked me into giving up some underpants I'd had since second grade. "Moving is a great time for getting rid of things you don't need," she told us.

The difference between Aunt Cis and Aunt Mavis is that Cis looks on the bright side of everything, while Mavis expects the worst to happen.

The thing is, Kathy," I heard Mavis saying to Mom, "here, at least, you know something about the kids your boys go around with. Celia's known their families for years. But when you move to a brand-new place, you don't know *who* their friends will be."

"That's the chance I've got to take, Mave."

"All it takes is one rotten apple to spoil the barrel," Aunt Mavis went on. "Kids can talk each other into anything."

"If Kathy's going to move, though, it's better she does it now," Keith put in. "Once Danny starts junior high, friends are more important than family, and you won't be able to tear him away."

I went on stuffing my underwear into a pillowcase, and wondered about Danny. I'd heard this talk before—

what Danny's going to be like in junior high, how he's going to change. I imagined his glands giving off some glue-like substance that attached him to friends. The Alien. The Creature from Outer Space. I looked over at Danny and grinned.

When I finished packing my clothes, I started in on our books, Danny's and mine. I picked up *From Boyhood to Manhood* that Grandma Flora, Dad's mom, had given Danny a while back. I held it up so Danny could see, and he started to laugh.

"Beware of false friends," we both said together, one of our favorite lines. Mom was laughing now.

"Should I pack this?" I asked.

"You'd better," she said. "Flora gave that to your dad when he was little. It used to be his father's, so it's a collector's item by now."

Danny used to read parts of it aloud to me at night and we'd roll off the bed laughing. There was a map in the front showing a little kid on the left side, with footprints leading to a picture of a grown man on the right. In between were "The Valley of Untruths" and "The Mountain of Cowardice" and "The River of Lust" that the boy had to cross before he could become a successful man. What really cracked us up was that the little kid had on a helmet labeled "Thrift" and boots labeled "Courage" and he was carrying a sword that said "Loyalty," and these were going to get him safely to the other side.

I stuck it in the box on top of some Batman comics and a Count Dracula doll that would clamp its fangs on your finger if you wound it up.

The next day, the movers picked up our storage furniture first, then came to Aunt Celia's to pick up the rest. Our friends rode over and sat balancing on their bikes while the men carried things out. I gave them all the games we didn't want, and they took everything but a checkerboard.

The hard part came that afternoon, saying good-bye to everyone. The guys just waved and rode away, which helped. But a woman across the street came over to see us off, and she just didn't know when to quit.

"Now let me have that address, Kathleen, so I can send a card on your birthday," she said to Mom. Then she grabbed my face between her hands and squeezed until my lips stuck out like fins. "Next time I see this boy, he'll have the big muscles, the mustache, even."

"It won't be *that* long!" said Mom. "We'll be coming back to visit Cis, remember."

Finally it was just Danny and me in the backseat, Mom in front, and Aunt Cis looking in the window.

"Danny, you take good care of your mother," she said, and I imagined us going off on safari somewhere, Danny fighting off tigers.

"I will," Danny told her.

"And T.R., let me hear from you now and then."

"Okay," I said.

The Chevy began to move. Aunt Cis blew us each a kiss, Mom tapped the horn, we rounded a corner, and were out of sight.

"Whew!" said Mom, and smiled in the rearview mirror.

Ever since Dad left, people have been telling Danny

that he's the Man of the House now. And he tries. Whenever Mom goes to a meeting at night, Danny waits up for her to make sure she gets home okay. He balances the checkbook for her, too, and once he tried to fix our toaster and almost electrocuted himself. I stood with one hand on the telephone, ready to dial 911 if I had to.

He looks out for Mom and I look out for Danny. But *From Boyhood to Manhood* hasn't been any help whatsoever.

It takes an hour and twenty minutes from Chicago to Rosemary Acres. Mom let Danny play whatever tapes he wanted, and it didn't seem like any time at all before we saw the blue shutters and gray doors that decorate all the townhouses in the development.

But right after we turned onto Cajun Drive, we saw something else: a huge bunch of balloons tied to the handle of our front door.

We stared.

"Grandma Flora, I'll bet," said Mom. "Flora or Cis, one or the other."

I was the first one out of the car and found the note with the balloons. "It's not from either one," I called. "It's from Dad."

Have a Happy! it read. *Love, Dad.*

Mom's pretty good about not bad-mouthing Dad—not to us, anyway. But this set her off.

"Thanks a lot," she muttered. "Did he give me balloons or flowers when you boys were born? How about when I got my master's degree or had my gall bladder

13

out? Now when we're trying to make a life without him, it seems a strange time to be sending greetings." And then, more softly, "Damn!"

I made a mental note that if I ever got married and my wife had her gall bladder out, I should send balloons.

Mom said she didn't care what we did with them, just get them out of the house, please, because she didn't want to be reminded of Dad every time she turned around. The movers weren't there yet, so Danny and I set off for the lake (Lake Tarragon, if you want to know), and found a spot that wasn't too bad. It was pretty nice, actually. The developer had managed to leave some trees and bushes down there, all in a clump at one end, so we headed for that.

I said we should send off all the balloons at once, but Danny wanted to let them go one at a time. We found a grassy place, lay down on our backs with our heads against a log, and each of us released a balloon at the same time, like a race, to see which one was first out of sight. There must have been sixteen or eighteen balloons altogether. We were saving the two Mylar hearts until last, those silver balloons with the messages, "Good Luck" and "Your Move."

Just as we were watching a race between a green one and a yellow one, I noticed somebody standing off to one side, and jerked my head around. There was that tall, skinny guy with the basketball fingers, watching.

I nudged Danny. He looked at the guy and grinned. The boy grinned back, then came over and put one foot on the log, watching the two balloons high overhead.

"You going to send the silver ones up, too?" he asked.

"Yeah," said Danny.

"Moving in?"

"We're waiting for the van to get here," I told him.

"I'm Paul Bremmer," the guy said.

"The Scarlino brothers," said Danny, with a smirk.

The Scarlino Brothers

Mom doesn't like for Danny to call us that. She says it sounds like the Mafia or something, and she wants us to remember that Italy also produced Marco Polo, Vespucci, Columbus, Verdi, Rossini, da Vinci, Boccaccio, Dante, Michelangelo, and the Pope. And then she adds that she's not mad at all Italians, just one of them.

Danny still calls us the Scarlino brothers, though, especially when he wants to sound a little tough.

Paul Bremmer was watching the balloons drift off in the sky. "You guys want to hang out down here some time?"

"Doing what?" Danny asked.

"Dad gave me this remote-control boat. It's sort of fun, you don't have anything else to do."

"Sure," Danny said.

"Sure," I echoed. I always go where Danny goes.

"Okay, see you around." And Paul loped off around the lake.

We could hear the grinding of the moving van up on Basil Boulevard, and wondered what the men were saying to each other about Parsley Place, Cinnamon Court, and Ginger Avenue. By the time all the balloons had floated away, we figured the movers had found Cajun Drive, so we walked back up to the house and they were already carrying stuff in.

Man, the muscles on those guys! One mover was carrying four kitchen chairs, two in each hand. I tried to help, jumping up in the van and digging around for stuff I could carry in. I felt like a nerd, though, walking in with a lampshade, especially when the head mover said, "You can help most, buddy, by just keeping out of the way."

The nice thing about Danny is he let me choose the bedroom I wanted. He said that since I'd be living in the house two years longer than he would, I should get first choice.

So I took one of the corner bedrooms. Mine had a tree—probably the only medium-sized tree in the whole development—just outside my window. I wondered if Rosemary, the builder's wife, was so sorry all the other trees were bulldozed that she chained herself to this one and said they'd have to take her, too, if they took the tree.

Danny and I showed the men where to put our beds and dressers. I opened a drawer of the dresser I hadn't seen for two years and found an old sock, some dead moths, and a Necco wafer. I think it was the sock that killed the moths.

After everything was in the house and the van left, the three of us got out the sandwiches Aunt Cis had packed and—because the table was piled high with boxes—ate an early supper on the living-room floor.

"Well," Mom said, her bare feet stuck out in front of her, with pearl-pink polish on her toenails. "Today is the first day of the rest of our lives."

I didn't answer. I missed Chicago already—all the noise. I never knew I'd miss noise so much—doors slamming, tires squealing, horns honking, men laughing, women talking, babies crying . . . . We had all the windows open, and even though I sat real still, the only thing I could hear from outside was a bird. One lousy bird.

"Penny for your thoughts, T.R. I'll even make it a quarter," Mom said. She was smiling at me, resting her head against the sofa. She's got curly, light brown hair, real bushy. Danny and I have thick hair, too, but it's black and wavy, more like Dad's.

I wished she'd asked Danny instead of me. Danny could think of an answer a lot faster.

"I guess I miss the guys. Aunt Cis and everybody," I said. I never was a very good liar.

"It's okay," Mom said. "I miss Cis, too. There are probably going to be a number of lonely days ahead, but you have to expect that whenever you make a big change. Things even out."

She sat quietly a moment, resting her Sprite can on one knee. Then she said, "Danny was really upset when we left that house on Dorchester and moved to Celia's.

But look how fast he made friends."

"I was upset?" Danny asked.

"You don't remember?"

"I was angry because Dad was leaving. I wasn't upset because we were going to Celia's."

"Whatever," said Mom.

"Why did he leave—really?" The words just came out before I could stop them. It's something we don't talk a lot about. Whenever I've asked in the past, Mom says things like, "We quarreled too much," or "It just seemed best to live apart."

But now Mom seemed to know it was time for the answer behind the answer. So she looked me right in the eye and said, "Because he fell in love with someone else."

Danny and I didn't move. I guess maybe way down inside I'd suspected that, but it was hard to know what to say. Mom seemed so relaxed, though, that I asked the obvious question: "Who?"

"A graduate student at the university."

The room was really quiet then. Even the lone bird outside had stopped chirping. But Danny was curious.

"Did you ever meet her, Mom?" he asked.

"No, and I never want to. End of conversation." Mom started to take another sip of Sprite, then put the can back down. "I'm sorry, that's not fair. If you have any more questions, let's talk about them."

I had a million questions, but none I could put into words. They all seemed too complicated. Finally Danny said, "Boy, I'm never going to get married."

"Why not?" Mom studied him.

"Because it's too risky." Danny sounded angry. "How do I know I'll never fall in love with someone else? There are girls all over the place. And how would I know *she* wouldn't like somebody better?"

"You don't. But even if you *are* tempted by someone else, the marriage should come first."

I felt really mad at my dad right then. "Dad's a college professor, Mom. Didn't he know better?"

"Oh, sweetie." Mom put out one hand and patted my knee. I hate it when she calls me sweetie. "Being smart in the classroom and being smart in life aren't the same thing. Believe me."

Danny and I put up our posters that night. We didn't have our books unpacked or our clothes put away—everything was still in bags and boxes along the walls. But once the posters were up, the rooms seemed more like ours. I had an old poster of *Jaws II*, another that Mom got at a book convention, showing a boy riding some prehistoric bird, and a couple more posters of Batman and Robin.

Danny's the one with the weird stuff, though. He has a few Far Side posters showing cows flying or cooking or dancing. He had another of a movie called *Eyes of the Dead* and an old calendar Uncle Keith gave him that Mom doesn't know about, of ladies in their underwear. Half their underwear, anyway.

The really neat thing, though, was that after we put up our posters, we opened some more pop and took it out on the patio, which overlooks both our little square of backyard and the whole lawn at the side. And we saw fireflies in the yard, probably more fireflies there in one evening than we saw in Chicago in one year.

I wondered what it was like to be a firefly. If you knew you lit up the night, I mean. Or whether you just went around with that big bulb in your backside set on automatic. I think about things like that.

In bed that night, I felt really strange—partly because Mom forgot where she'd packed the sheets, so I was lying on my bare mattress, partly because I'd always slept in the same room with Danny before, and also because I just didn't see how I could ever like it out here at Rosemary Acres. It was just too . . . too *new* or something.

I got up finally and went to the doorway of Danny's room.

"I feel weird," I said.

Danny was almost asleep. He didn't move for a minute, then raised himself up on one elbow. "You sick?"

"I feel strange."

"If you're going to throw up, T.R., go in the bathroom."

I sat down on the edge of his bed. "No, I'm just not sure I'm going to like it here . . ." I swallowed.

"It's not forever," Danny said. "Only till we go to college." That didn't help a bit. I was feeling sort of panicky, like maybe we'd made the wrong decision. "Maybe we should tell Mom it was a big mistake, and we want to go back and live with Aunt Cis. If it turned out that I'm allergic to the house or something—I mean, if one of us got sneezing fits—couldn't we get our money back?"

I was all ready to do it, too—have sneezing fits—but Danny's pretty good at talking you out of something stupid. Sometimes, anyway. I remember once, just before Mom and Dad separated, I knew Dad wasn't going to give her anything for her birthday, so I'd ordered this black nightgown from a catalog, and was going to wrap it up and sign Dad's name. But Danny told me she'd know, because I'd ordered a 38, and that's about three sizes too big. (I'd picked 38 because that's how old Mom was then, but Danny said you don't buy women's clothes that way. If you did, Grandma Flora would be wearing a 70 or something.) Danny said that he and I should take her out to dinner instead, so that's what we'd done.

"Anyway, T.R., Mom likes this house," Danny was saying now. "It really means a lot to her. She'll be able to go out if she wants without Aunt Cis always knowing about it."

I swallowed again. "Well, I don't know what it is, Danny, but everything seems too new."

He turned over on his back and put his arms behind his head. I could see his face in the moonlight. "That's it, I guess."

It helped to be able to pinpoint what was wrong. I pulled up my legs and crossed them. "Everything shines," I said. "The lampposts, the doorknobs. . . ."

"Right."

"And all the rooms smell like fresh paint and new carpets."

"Yeah."

"Nothing's natural," I went on, really getting into it. "Nothing except that clump of trees down by the lake. Everything's been built, even the lake."

Danny nodded. "The sidewalks are white and smooth. The curbs are smooth. No cracks. It's like a movie set."

We were really cooking now. "And you hardly hear any noise," I put in. "A couple crickets, maybe. One bird, a few—"

I stopped. Danny turned his head toward the window. There was a distant *thunk . . . thunk . . . thunk.* And somehow we knew that over on the next street, down at the end of the block, Paul Bremmer was out there in the moonlight, shooting baskets by himself.

Cow-Pattie Bingo

The next day we discovered we had no mailbox. It was Saturday, and we all slept until eleven. As soon as we'd had breakfast, Mom said, "T.R., see if we've got any mail."

I poked my head out the front door and looked both ways—no box. I pulled on my jeans, walked barefoot to the end of our sidewalk, and looked around.

The entrance of each townhouse was shielded slightly from the others. If one was up a few steps, the next was down. In some places there were even a few feet of fence between entrances, so you couldn't see your neighbor go in or out. Like we all worked for the CIA or something. I looked up and down the whole street.

"No boxes," I said when I went back inside.

"None at all?" Mom couldn't believe it, and went outside herself. She hadn't been there five seconds before she was having a conversation with someone.

You can put Mom on a perfectly deserted street, and within seconds somebody pops up out of a manhole or something.

When she came back in, she said, "Guess what?"

"There is no other life on this planet," said Danny.

Mom gave him her patient look. "All the mailboxes for each block are together at the corner. If you guys can't think of anything better to do, walk over to the office and ask for the key to ours."

There wasn't anything better to do, so Danny put on his sleeveless T-shirt and some shorts, and we set off.

The sun was really bright, and everything that had seemed to gleam the day before positively shone now. No shade anywhere. There were a few more people out this time, washing their cars or sweeping the sidewalk, but mostly they kept to themselves. It wasn't like in Chicago where every time you stepped out the front door you said hi.

The mailboxes were on each corner like the neighbor said—a big bank of them, one on top of another in rows. At the office, Miss Quinn told us that if you got a package, you'd find a second key in your box, and this would open the bin at the end where the packages were placed. It seemed to me that this whole community was designed so that nobody would have to talk to anyone else, not even the mailman.

"Don't fool around with that key now. Take it right home," Miss Quinn told us.

Danny stopped, and I could tell he was about to say something smart. I nudged him with my elbow and got him out of there just in time. Like a good sheepdog, I have to look out for Danny.

"If she hadn't warned me, I might have swallowed it," said Danny.

But then we discovered that right behind the office was a community center with a meeting room and an outdoor swimming pool. Nobody was in either of them, of course, except for one old man in flowered jams floating about on an inner tube, hands over his stomach.

"No other *intelligent* life on this planet," Danny said.

We walked through the meeting room, and up on one wall was this huge bulletin board with notes about things to sell, or people who needed baby-sitters. Danny was reading one that advertised a used trail bike when I noticed a big yellow sign in one corner:

Rosemary Acres Residents
"MEET-YOUR-NEIGHBOR-SUNDAY"
July 3, 2:00 p.m.
Hillman's Farm (north of development)
"Cow-Pattie Bingo"
Cola, Popcorn, and Ice Cream
Everybody Welcome

I knew I ought to get Danny there—to meet other people, I mean. If he made new friends out here at Rosemary Acres, he'd be less likely to take up with drug addicts when he got to junior high school, and Aunt Mavis could stop worrying.

"Hey, Danny," I said. "You want some cola, popcorn, ice cream, and cow patties?"

Danny looked at the sign and started to grin.

"Wanna go?" I asked.

"Why not?" he said.

Mom said the same thing when we asked her. "It's a good way to meet people," she added. And then she did a double take: "Cow-pattie *bingo*?"

Hillman's farm backed right up against Rosemary Acres. Mom and I figured that Mr. Hillman wanted to be friends with the people in the development so they wouldn't steal his sweet corn in August, and the management at Rosemary Acres wanted to stay on good terms with Mr. Hillman so if he ever sold his property, he'd sell it to them. By the time we got to the farm the next day, management had set up a long table with cold drinks and popcorn, and had hired a Good Humor truck for the occasion. All we had to pay for was the ice cream.

You want to hear weird? A whole section of pasture behind the barn had been fenced off, and someone had taken white paint and divided it into squares, all of them numbered like a bingo card. What was going to happen, see, was that Mr. Hillman would let a cow into the pasture, and wherever it dropped a pattie, that was the winning square.

There were name tags that read, "Hello, I'm _____," and pens to write your name; there were red kerchiefs for everyone to wear around their necks, to look like hayseeds, and there was a big plastic fishbowl with numbers in it—five numbers for every square in the pasture, they told us. You drew a number, and if the cow pooped in your square, you and four other people got ten bucks apiece. I mean, somebody actually sat down and thought this thing up.

Danny and I took our Coke and popcorn and leaned against the fence to the cow pasture. We'd put on name tags but not the red kerchiefs. The adults all wore them, though, and as soon as they put them on, they got silly. Some of the men acted as though they didn't know the kerchiefs went around their necks, and tied them around their heads instead. The women all laughed. There were lots of grown-ups, a bunch of little kids climbing around over some bales of hay, and a lot of yuppies, but hardly anyone my age and Danny's.

"This really sucks," said Danny.

Paul Bremmer sauntered over. He doesn't really saunter as much as he lopes, and doesn't lope as much as he glides—like he's on wheels or something.

"Hi," I said when I saw him. Then I looked at his name tag. It said, "Hello, I'm Clem."

"Clem?" said Danny. We laughed.

"You got a number?" Paul asked us as he leaned on the fence beside us. His arms stuck out several inches farther than ours. "I've got seventeen."

"I've got six, Danny's got eleven," I told him.

We studied the giant bingo diagram there in the pasture.

"Whole thing seems pretty iffy to me," said Paul. He had a long face to fit his body, and there was a lot of space, I noticed, between his nose and upper lip. "If the cow's constipated, and there isn't any pattie, you think they'll issue rain checks?"

Danny and I grinned.

"What if it's got the runs and hits half a dozen spaces?" Danny suggested.

This time Paul and I laughed.

"It would be udder chaos," said Paul, and we really guffawed.

Mom was helping out at the registration table, making sure everybody had a name tag, and I was glad because that meant Danny and I didn't have to stick close by to see that she was enjoying herself.

"Is this what people here do for excitement?" Danny asked Paul.

"I don't know. I've only been here a month."

"Yeah?"

"Me and dad," Paul said.

Somebody was leading a cow out of the barn, and people started clapping. Mr. Hillman, the farmer, smiled, unlatched the gate to the pasture, and everybody moved toward the fence. I wondered if Mr. Hillman had spent the morning in the barn watching the cows so he could choose the one most likely to succeed.

When the cow was alone in the marked field, the crowd started yelling.

"Go for number three!" somebody called.

"No! Eight, bossy, eight!"

"Make it nineteen, honey."

"Seven!"

"Twenty-six!"

The cow stood absolutely still, its huge brown eye staring sideways at the crowd, its tail going from side to side. It took a few steps and stopped again.

I couldn't help wondering how I'd feel if I was that cow. I could just imagine myself about a hundred times heavier, standing out in the field on all fours, everyone waiting for me to poop. Mom says when I was small, I told everyone I was a puppy. She said I used to drive Aunt Mavis crazy by licking her cheek.

"Fourteen! Fourteen! Fourteen!" chanted some people across from us.

"Stay right there, baby!" a woman yelled. "You're doing just fine."

The cow went a few steps farther and peed.

"No, no, folks, that doesn't count," Mr. Hillman told the crowd.

"I can't believe I'm doing this," Paul said to us. "I can't believe I'm spending a perfectly good Sunday waiting for some cow to do her business."

It looked as though we were going to be there all afternoon. The cow spent the next ten minutes eating grass. Sometimes she'd lift her head and fix her eye on somebody when the crowd got restless and began to shout or chant, but she'd go right on chewing and swishing her tail. She walked from square nineteen to fourteen, made a left and edged into eleven, then moved out again, and rubbed her head against the fence.

Just when we thought we'd be waiting all afternoon, though, the cow sidled over into square twenty-three, lifted her tail, and let go. Five people holding tickets for square twenty-three jumped up and down like idiots. Mr. Hillman told the crowd that if the cow did an encore within the next five minutes, he'd honor a second square. Everybody clapped for Mr. Hillman.

I glanced over at Danny and Paul, but they weren't even watching the cow. I turned to see what they were staring at, and saw a girl in cutoffs, with freckles all over her arms and legs, eating an Eskimo pie, and coming right down the path toward us.

The Talking Porta-John

I thought maybe Paul knew her—his cousin or something. Then I realized he didn't, because she walked right on by. We managed to see her name tag. Mickey, it read.

"Mouse?" Paul asked out loud, grinning.

She gave him a look and kept going, and he and Danny turned slowly around like the figurines on top of a music box.

"Wow!" breathed Danny. "Even her freckles are cute."

"She looks like a gorgeous speckled egg," agreed Paul.

Danny was grinning again. "I'd sure like to scramble that egg," he said, and he and Paul laughed.

"How about eggs over light?" said Paul, and he and Danny laughed some more.

I didn't know what they were talking about, but I said, "I like my eggs poached."

Paul and Danny looked at me, but nobody laughed. I say lots of stupid things sometimes.

I wonder if she lives in Rosemary Acres," said Danny. "If we knew her last name, we could check the mailboxes and find out where she lives."

"Go ask her," I said.

"Naw," said Danny.

And suddenly I knew what I could do for my brother. I could go ask her myself. What was so hard about that?

"I'll go," I said.

Danny and Paul both stared at me, then grinned, and I took off after the girl with the freckled legs. I was going to miss watching the cow do an encore, but I didn't care.

As far back as I can remember, Danny's been the one to do everything first—to test the water, explore the territory, you might say, especially after Dad left. When we went sledding at Grandpa Gil's up in Wisconsin, Danny always went down the hill first, to see if there were any bumps or holes.

He was the one who had to wrangle with Mom about stretching bedtime from nine to ten, so that by the time I wanted to stay up until eleven on weekends, it was no problem. It was Danny who cut holes in his jeans first and got heck for it, Danny who got that sex book out of the library so I could see the pictures. Danny, always Danny, who made his way across the mine fields while I waited back home.

This time it was me going out on reconnaissance, and Danny and Paul waiting back at camp. More than that, I knew how pleased Aunt Cis and Aunt Mavis would be if I could tell them that Danny already had a girlfriend.

The girl with the speckled legs had walked into the

crowd, and I plunged in after her. For a moment I thought I'd lost her. But when I came out on the other side, I saw her going up the sloping lawn—the faded cutoffs, the red T-shirt, and the ribbon holding up her hair in back. I guess I liked speckled eggs, too.

She stopped once and looked over her shoulder. I wondered if she knew I was following her.

Now, I told myself. Just go up and ask her what her last name is. But then I thought how stupid that sounded, and decided I'd better rehearse it first. You just don't go up to a girl and say, "What's your last name?" I knew Paul and Danny would ask me everything I'd said, and I didn't want it to sound as dumb as, "I like my eggs poached."

Besides, the girl had started off again, so I followed about thirty feet behind. Maybe I could ask if she lived at Rosemary Acres, and how was the pool. Yeah, I could start off like that.

Mickey was walking faster, and I didn't know if I only imagined it, but she seemed to be weaving in and out of trees on purpose. Every so often I saw her glance at me over her shoulder.

She knows! I thought. She knows I've been following her! I've got to go right up there and talk to her before she gets away! But as soon as I started going faster, she began to jog, her ponytail bouncing up and down.

Jeez! I thought. This was so dumb! What if Paul and Danny were watching? They'd bend over double laughing.

Okay, this was it, I decided. I ran as fast as I could, and when I was only six feet behind her, she ran into a

Porta-John and closed the door.

I skidded to a stop and stared. The Porta-John had a little figure of a woman on it. About twenty feet away, under a sycamore tree, was another Porta-John with a figure of a man on it. What the heck did I do now?

The cow must have done an encore down in the pasture, because the crowd was clapping and cheering. There was music coming out of loudspeakers, and a few of the yuppies, in their pressed shirts and shorts, started to dance.

A woman came by and stared hard at me. "The boys' is over there," she said, nodding toward the other toilet.

"I know," I said uncomfortably.

The woman raised her eyebrows, then went on.

This is so dumb, I told myself, my face growing hotter by the minute. T.R., you are so stupid! Why didn't you just go up to her right at the first and ask her her last name?

Two more women came by and looked at me in the same way, and I decided I was standing too close to the women's john. So I walked a few feet more and turned away, my hands in my pockets, rocking back and forth on my heels.

What was she doing in there? Why didn't I hear a flush? Then I realized there wouldn't be any flush in a Porta-John.

I edged back again, listening. No noises at all. And then I saw her down by the ice-cream truck—the red T-shirt, the cutoffs. I stared. How had she gotten out without my seeing her? She must have been watching me through the keyhole and left as soon as I turned my back.

I stared at the Porta-John. It didn't have a keyhole.

"T.R., you're a jerk!" I said out loud, starting away, furious at myself. "See what happens when you. . . ."

"Hey, boy, you always go around talking to yourself?"

I whirled about. No one was there. It was really eerie. I walked all around the Porta-John to see if someone was hiding behind it.

"You know, you're sort of kinky," the voice came again, "hanging around a girls' john."

It was coming from the top of the portable toilet, from a little screened window just under the roof. It was like the talking telephone booth in the commercials.

"You do this a lot? Follow girls into bathrooms?" the voice continued.

"Hey, look!" I said. "I just wanted to find out who she was, that's all."

"T.R.?"

I whirled again. Danny and Paul were coming up behind me.

"What'd you find out?" Paul asked.

I grabbed Danny's arm and pointed. "It . . . it was talking!" I said.

Paul looked at me strangely.

"Honest! I followed her here, and somehow she got out without my knowing. She's down there, and all at once the john started talking to me!"

Danny and Paul looked at the Porta-John. Nothing happened. I could feel the blood rushing to my face. I felt like King of the Nerds.

"*Say* something!" I yelled, and kicked the john.

"Ouch!" said the voice, followed by a giggle.

"There's someone in there," whispered Danny.

"But she's over there!" I pointed toward the Good Humor truck. And then I saw a girl in a red shirt and blue cutoffs, walking with friends near the popcorn table. Only that girl didn't have a ponytail.

"You know, all three of you guys are a little kinky," the voice from the Porta-John said again, and all at once the door swung open and out came Mickey. The three of us stared, arms hanging at our sides, as she jogged down the slope to the cow pasture, laughing all the way.

That almost ruined the Fourth of July. Danny wasn't so upset that I didn't find out her last name as he was that Mickey probably thought we were all jerks.

But then Grandpa Gil drove down from Milwaukee to see our new house. I was really glad he'd come, because just when Danny and I were complaining that there was no place to watch fireworks, Grandpa Gil got out a sack he'd stowed behind the couch.

"Dad, what in the world is that?" Mom asked.

"Now you just go right on with your unpacking, Kathleen, because the boys and I have a little business to take care of," Gramps said. "Where're your matches?"

Mom laughed and gave them to him. "I'm coming, too," she said, and the four of us went out on the back steps to open Gramps's sack.

He must have bought out half a store. There were fireworks I'd never even heard of. No sparklers for

Grandpa Gil. There were not only tricolored rockets, but snakes, spinners, tweeters, crawlers, sunbursts, and galaxies.

We started off with the snakes and crawlers, and when we got to spinners and rockets, we moved out to the folding chairs on the side lawn. Only a couple of kids were watching at first. Then Paul Bremmer showed up, a few parents with small children, and by the time a sunburst exploded in the sky, there was a crowd of neighbors sitting on the grass in the dark, clapping.

I was sorry that Aunt Celia wasn't there. Aunt Cis is always nice to have around when you're having fun, because she manages to have the most fun of all. But I was secretly glad that Aunt Mavis and Uncle Lyle hadn't come, because Aunt Mave would have said that fireworks were too dangerous, that someone could get a cinder in the eye. Then she would have told us the story of some kid who lost a finger lighting a firecracker, and if that didn't scare us, she would have told the story again, only this time the boy would have lost his whole hand.

It was a quarter to ten when management called. Miss Quinn told Mom she'd been gone all day, and had just got back, and didn't we know that there was a county ordinance against fireworks? Mom thanked her for telling us, and said we had only two more galaxies to go, and Miss Quinn said she was sorry, but there would be no more fireworks of any kind permitted.

What happened was that the two galaxies went off anyway, and when the crowd was breaking up to go home, Miss Quinn came marching up our sidewalk.

"I can't believe that even after I called, you continued to set those off," she told Mom.

Mom smiled. "I just didn't get outside in time to stop Dad," she explained.

"It's clearly against the law, and sets a bad example for the children."

"Oh, Miss Quinn," said Mom, "Dad's in his seventies. Can't we humor him a little?"

Miss Quinn paused, and for a moment I thought she was giving in. "Look, we're trying very hard to make Rosemary Acres a safe, attractive place to live," she said. "And I would appreciate the cooperation of *all* our families." Then she turned and walked back up the sidewalk. She was wearing a red, white, and blue skirt for the Fourth of July, but she looked like about as much fun as a glass of lemon juice. I'd bet my allowance that it wasn't Miss Quinn who thought up cow-pattie bingo.

She reminded me a lot of my fourth-grade teacher. Last year we were studying the pioneers, and for six weeks my teacher talked about how hard life was on the prairie. We had a Pioneer Day and we all had to wear something scratchy so we'd know what it felt like to wear pioneer clothes. For that whole day we had to sit on benches without backs so we'd know what it was like in a pioneer school, and for lunch, all we could have was cornbread and berries. It was one of the most miserable days of my life, and I've always believed that our teacher just liked to see us suffer.

"What a sourpuss!" Danny said, watching Quinn go.

"Oh, she probably hasn't been around children very much," Gramps said. "Give her time. She'll mellow out."

Mom went back to unpacking all our books and putting them on the shelves—she said she wanted to get that done before bedtime, so Danny and I sat on the back steps a while longer with Gramps.

Gilbert's his real name, Gilbert Fitzpatrick. He was an Irish Protestant who married an Irish Catholic, and he said the only thing he and Grandma Fitzpatrick didn't argue about was religion, because they'd made a promise not to. It must have worked, because they had three children along the way—Mom, Mavis, and Keith, and stayed married right up to the day Grandma Fitzpatrick died.

"Well," Grandpa Gil said as we watched the fireflies take over where the fireworks had been. "You boys think you're going to like it out here in the country?"

That was the first time I'd thought of Rosemary Acres as country. I hadn't thought of it as city either. In fact, I hadn't thought of it as village or suburb or anything much at all—just a development that smelled of fresh paint, and hardly had any trees.

"I don't know," I said honestly. "It's too early to tell."

"Give it a little time," said Grandpa. "Things'll even out."

That must be one of the favorite sayings of the Irish.

Then Gramps went down to sleep in our family room, on the same hide-a-bed that Danny and I had been sleeping on at Aunt Celia's. We showed him how to open it without hurting his back, and a handful of pretzels fell out. Danny and I went upstairs to the old beds we had missed for two years, and the nice thing about going to sleep that night was that a faint whiff of firecracker smoke still lingered in my room. So far we'd found one friend for Danny, I was thinking, but I'd have to work some to add Mickey to the list.

The Master Detective

It was about four days later, after Grandpa Gil had gone back to Milwaukee, that I saw Mickey again, about seven in the evening. I was out riding my bike around the development, wondering if I could smell clover, the way Mom said, and trying to memorize which streets connected with what. And suddenly, there she was, walking along Coriander. Before I was even close enough to see her freckles, I could tell it was Mickey.

This time, I told myself, I wasn't going to lose my chance. I wasn't going to rehearse. I wasn't even going to think about what to say, because if I did I'd get cold feet. Everything depended on my finding out her name. If Danny had a girlfriend here at Rosemary Acres, he wouldn't go looking for bad apples, and if a drug dealer came up to him while he was walking with his arm around Mickey and asked, "You want to buy some dope?" Danny would tell him to get lost. I could almost hear him say it. "Get lost, man!" Just like that.

I started pedaling faster and faster, my heart going like a bongo, until I was right alongside her, and suddenly I pulled directly in front of her and stopped.

Mickey stood dead still. She didn't smile, didn't frown—she just studied me like some curious sort of bug that had dropped from the sky.

"Mickey," I said, "I'm sorry about following you the other day. All I wanted was to find out your last name. If you don't tell me, I'm mashed potatoes, dead meat, road kill." I never knew I was so eloquent.

Mickey took a few steps as though she were going to walk around behind my bike, but I backed up.

"Just tell me your last name," I pleaded.

This time her eyes started to crinkle at the corners, and then her lips parted into a smile.

"What's yours?" she asked.

"Scarlino. T.R. Scarlino."

"What does the T.R. stand for?"

"Nothing. Well, not yet. I'm supposed to pick out a name when I'm grown."

"Neat!" said Mickey.

"Please," I said. "Just tell me what your last name is so I can tell Danny and Paul."

"Those other two guys?"

"Yeah. Danny's my brother—the one with the black hair."

"Harris," she said, and tapped my fender with one fingernail. "May I go now?"

"Sure!" I grinned and moved out of the way. "Thanks, Mickey."

I tore home like I was carrying state secrets to Washington, dropped my bike on the front steps, and burst into the house.

"I got it!" I yelled, running upstairs. "I got it, Danny! It's Harris!"

Danny was reading the sports section, and had papers strewn all over the place.

"What are you talking about?"

"Mickey's last name!" I panted, collapsing on the edge of his bed. "It's . . . Harris. I just . . . caught up with her . . . and found out." I was gasping.

"Well? Where does she live?"

I was speechless.

Danny looked exasperated. "You didn't find out? You got her last name but didn't find out where she lives?"

I couldn't believe I was such an idiot. I stared down at the rug and shook my head.

Danny must have known how I felt because he said, more gently, "Did you at least notice what street she was on?"

"Coriander. That's all I know," I told him.

He patted me on the shoulder. "Well, it's a start. It's okay."

Right at that moment, though, I didn't feel like being patted. I wondered if that's why dogs snap at you sometimes. And suddenly I forgot all about why Mickey was important. She was a jerk, that's what! What kind of girl would tell you her last name without telling you where she lived?

"Who cares where Mickey lives anyway?" I snarled,

shrugging his hand off. "Who cares what her last name is?" Danny was standing up now, picking up the pages of the newspaper. "You want a girlfriend with freckled legs who climbs up on toilet seats and calls dumb things out the window?" I croaked.

Danny left the room and started downstairs. I guess he *did* want a girlfriend with freckled legs who climbed up on toilet seats. Well, he could have her. He and Paul could fight over her, if they wanted. What teed me off was that Paul had promised to take his remote-control boat down to the lake sometime, and now that he'd met Mickey, he'd forgotten all about it. I went to the top of the stairs.

"And tell Paul if he doesn't want his boat, he can give it to me, because I don't care if Mickey's got freckles on her legs," I yelled. "I don't care if she has freckles on her butt. I don't care if she has freckles on her tits—"

Down below, Mom appeared around the corner of the living room. "T.R.?" she said.

Danny glanced at me over his shoulder.

"Who are you two talking about?" Mom asked.

"Nobody," said Danny, and went outside.

I didn't see much of Danny the rest of the day. He and Paul went riding around Rosemary Acres on their bikes, and didn't come back till evening. Mom was putting up shelf paper in all the closets, and had left tacos on the table for us. Paul stayed for supper, and the three of us ate together. I sat pulling all the lettuce out of my tacos.

"Well," I said finally, "did you find her?"

"No," Danny told me. "We checked every mailbox in the whole development, and there's not a Harris on any of them."

"So she's a freckled liar," I said.

"Don't be stupid," said Paul.

I didn't like the way Paul said that. He didn't have any right to call me stupid, and I wasn't so sure I liked him just then. What did we really know about him, anyway? His name and where he lived. Big deal. I got up and clumped outside. But once I was on the steps, I thought about it some more. What if Paul didn't work out? I mean, what if Paul himself turned out to be a bad apple and Danny didn't have any other friends in the development? I *had* to find out where Mickey lived, so I rode my bike over to Coriander, the place I'd seen Mickey last.

I sat down on the curb, my back against a retaining wall that was holding back a bank of pansies, and decided I'd wait right there till it got dark. I'd get up the next day and come out there and sit, and the day after that, until Mickey Harris came down the street again. Then I felt mad all over again. When I saw Mickey the next time, I was going to tell her what I thought of girls who hide in Porta-Johns and lie about their names. I could forgive her for making me look like a jerk, but I couldn't forgive her for causing trouble between Danny and me.

After only ten minutes, though, I saw some people come out of a townhouse down the street, and one of them was Mickey. I couldn't see her freckles, but I could tell it was her by the dark hair, held up in back by a ribbon, by the way she walked, the shape of her chin. . . .

She and her family, I guess, were saying goodbye to a couple who were getting in a car, and after the car drove off, some of the people went back inside, but Mickey sat out on the steps, holding a baby in her lap.

I got on my bike and rode over.

Mickey had on a full skirt, and it hung down between her knees, making a sort of swing for the baby. The kid himself was ugly. He was about one, I guess, and was probably teething, because he was slobbering all over the place.

"Well, if it isn't the Master Detective!" Mickey said when she saw me, and went on swinging the baby back and forth in her skirt.

I left my bike at the fence and came halfway up the walk.

"You can sit here on the steps. I won't bite. This is Gus," Mickey said, showing off the baby. "He's why we moved here. We needed more room."

"Whose is he?" I cautiously sat down on a step just below hers.

"Mom's."

"Then how come Danny and Paul couldn't find any Harris on any of the mailboxes?"

She looked at me in surprise, and then her eyes were laughing again. "You've been trying to find out where I live, right?"

"Wrong. *Danny's* been trying to find you. I don't like girls who lie."

Mickey stopped rocking the ugly baby. "Listen, T.R., I didn't lie. I'm Mickey Harris, and I live with my mom and stepdad, a stepbrother and a half brother." She glanced at Gus. "Their names are Freeman, but I'm still a Harris."

Man, and I thought our family was mixed up.

She was smiling again. "If I'd known you were going to be looking for me, I would have told you to look for Freeman." She laughed. "Maybe."

I decided I liked Mickey right then. Liked her a lot, in fact. Suddenly the baby started to slip out of her skirt and onto the steps. Mickey lunged for him, and as she bent over, I couldn't help but notice she had freckles as far as I could see.

Danny and Paul were up in Danny's room trying to work one of those metal tavern puzzles that Keith had given us at Christmas. Double Trouble, this one was called, and it was a dilly. No one had got it yet.

I just leaned against the door frame. "Two eighty-three Coriander Street," I said. "Mickey Harris lives with her mom, her stepdad, a stepbrother, and a half brother, but *their* last name is Freeman." And then, as an afterthought, I added, "And she really does have freckles on her tits."

I went into my room, lay down on my bed, and turned the radio on. Danny and Paul came and stood in the doorway, staring at me, their mouths half open, but I just went on grinning, tapping one foot to the music.

Moses and Me

The thing about Danny and Paul was that they didn't do anything. After the trouble I went to to find out where Mickey lived, all they did was ride by there a million times on their bikes. They didn't even go knock on the door. Mickey was probably watching out a window all the time. Sometimes I don't understand Danny.

But I understood enough to know that one friend isn't enough to keep you out of trouble, and that back in Chicago, Aunt Cis was probably concerned about how we were getting along in Rosemary Acres, and down in Florida, Grandma Flora was probably praying to some saint to protect us, and over in Evanston, Aunt Mavis was certainly worried about us, and probably thought that by now Danny and I were out stealing car radios. I had to round up some new friends somehow, but you can't exactly advertise. Danny, I figured, was good-looking enough that he could get a girl on his own if he tried. I don't think he was trying, though.

Mom says we both look like Dad. I've got a picture in my scrapbook of Dad holding me when I was four. He's tall in the picture, handsome, real dark, wavy hair, like ours, a long straight nose, and white teeth. He's smiling, and his teeth look great.

It's weird, but you know what I remember most about my dad? His car. It wasn't any fancy kind of car. It was silver gray and had a hood ornament that looked like a star with all the points connected. Dad used to let me help him wash it, and I'd always do the headlights, the hubcaps, and the hood ornament.

I just liked being in that car. I liked Dad's sunglasses holder up on the visor, the tape deck, the old umbrella Dad kept on the floor in the back, the smell of the upholstery, and Dad's after-shave. Whenever I think about my dad, I think about his car. But every time I think about his car, I remember what happened in it, and then I feel sick.

We were all in the car that day. I don't remember where we were going, but Danny and I were horsing around in the backseat. Danny had a grip on my arm and had wrestled me to the floor. I was laughing, but Dad said if we didn't buckle up right away, he was going to pull over and stop.

So Danny let go of me and I started to get up, and then I said, "Hey, Mom, I found one of your earrings," and I picked up a gold circle with a wire on the back that was under the seat on the passenger side. I passed it up to Mom, and she said, "That's not mine."

I was lying in bed the other night thinking how that's

all she said, just those three words, and a month after that, our folks separated. I used to think, If only I hadn't found it, if I'd just tossed it out the window or something. If I'd just kept my mouth shut, maybe the whole thing would have blown over.

I told Danny what I'd been thinking, and he said no, that Mom probably suspected all along that Dad had been dating his graduate assistant, and that the earring was only added proof. I said, "Well, maybe he was just driving her home on a rainy day," and Danny said, "Wanna bet?"

We hadn't been in our townhouse long when we got a call from Grandma Flora.

"Kathleen, I'm coming," she said. Mom always holds the phone away from her ear, because Grandma talks so loud, and everyone else in the room can hear.

"Oh, Flora, this place is a mess. We're still unpacking, I haven't cleaned the bathrooms, there's dust. . . ."

"You think I don't know mess? You think I don't know dust? That's why I wanna come, Kathleen, give you a hand."

Mom sighed and smiled at the same time. "Okay, Flora," she said. "When's your plane?"

"Flora, from Florida!" Mom said, holding out her arms, and Dad's mother walked right into them and hugged Mom like she was her own daughter.

Grandma Flora doesn't look anything like the Italian grandmothers in spaghetti advertisements. Her hair is black and silver and she wears it short. She's thin, and dresses nice, too. The only thing about her I don't like are her shoes—orthopedic things with arch supports. When she saw me looking at them once she said, "Only my feet are old, T.R.," and I was embarrassed.

It took almost fifteen minutes to get out of O'Hare, not to mention the drive back, and all the way home, Grandma Flora kept taking things out of her carry-on bag to show what she'd brought—mostly stuff she'd had in her refrigerator and hadn't wanted to leave behind. So lunch that day was zucchini bread, provolone cheese, sausage and pasta, a couple of chicken breasts, and some strawberries.

She set right to work. She put her bags by the hide-a-bed, changed into pants and a shirt, and by the time lunch was over and the dishes were in the sink, we could hear Grandma vacuuming the rug in the family room and singing.

We were having a snack together that afternoon out on the patio, Grandma and I. More zucchini bread with some lemonade, and just out of the blue, I asked her, "Do you still like Dad?"

The thing about Grandma Flora is she never acts surprised, no matter what you ask. "Of course," she said. "He's my son, no matter what."

I thought that over while I chewed. "Would you like him even if he went out and killed a hundred people?"

"He didn't," said Grandma.

"But what if he did?"

"But he didn't." And then she added, "You can like a

person and not like what he does. What Thomas did, I don't like."

"Why do you think he's never come back to see Danny and me?" That was my real question, I guess.

"That I especially don't like," Grandma said. But she didn't have an answer.

Danny and I figured he was too embarrassed. A couple of months after he and Mom separated, Dad had a sabbatical—that's like a long vacation, where you're supposed to do research or something—and he took his graduate assistant to Greece for a year. Danny and I got postcards from Athens and Crete, and Dad even sent us Greek sailor caps, only mine was too big.

After he got back, he wrote to Danny and said he'd accepted a professorship at Berkeley, and did Danny and I want to see him before he moved to California?

"So why did he send a letter? He's back in Chicago. Why the heck doesn't he call?" Danny had said.

What happened was that Danny put off writing him back, and I guess Dad figured that meant no, because the next thing we heard, he was in California. Another year went by with only postcards now and then. Maybe if you go two years without seeing your kids, it gets harder and harder to try. I'll bet he thinks of us, though. Grandma Flora passes on all the news about us, and that's why he sent the balloons.

In the kitchen later, I heard Mom and Grandma talking.

"That girl's gone, Kathleen."

"Well, if one's gone, you can be sure he's got another."

"How do you know this? How long you gonna go, no

letters, no phone calls? He's a proud man, that's all, don't wanna take the first step."

"Well, I'm a proud woman," Mom told her. "I wouldn't take Tom back if he came with a guarantee."

"You don't miss him, even a little?"

"Sometimes I miss him more than a little, Flora, but it doesn't help, does it?"

"So maybe you just stay friends! Lady I knew in New York, she and her husband been separated seventeen years. Seventeen years, Kathleen! And every Sunday, he drives out to Long Island to take her the *Times*."

"That's sick, Flora."

"In God's eyes, you're still married, you know, you and Tom."

"Well, God didn't have to live with him. I did."

Danny and I are religious ignoramuses, according to Grandma Flora.

"Kathleen, I don't like to interfere . . . ," Grandma said.

"Then don't," Mom kidded her, as always, but Grandma went right ahead.

"Raise your boys Catholic, Kathleen, or raise them Protestant. But raise them knowing the Lord."

"They went to Sunday school when they were little—Danny did, anyway," said Mom.

Danny and I were trying to read the comics over our cereal. Mom was at one end of the table, Grandma at the other. I looked across at Danny and smiled, then went back to Spider-Man again. But Spider-Man can't compete with Grandma Flora.

"Danny, who's Cain?" Grandma asked.

"Give me a break," said Danny. "The guy who killed Abel."

"Sampson?"

"The dude with the hair."

I stared. I'd never heard of either of them. Then Grandma concentrated on me: "T.R., who's Moses?"

My first thought was Moses Malone, the basketball player, but I knew he wouldn't do. Moses and the bulrushes, I thought. Where had I heard that? What the heck were bulrushes?

"The guy with the tablets," Danny murmured under his breath, then took a big slurp of cereal.

But Grandma heard. "No coaching," she said. Then, to me, "You don't know Moses?"

I shook my head. Grandma Flora shook hers.

"What happened on Mount Ararat?" she asked. The questions were coming like shotgun pellets. I didn't know if this was geography or history.

"Some kind of battle?" I guessed.

"Noah," Danny whispered. "Noah and the ark."

"On a *mountain*?" I said out loud, forgetting.

"You flunk," said Grandma.

"For your information, Flora, I'm thinking of bringing them up Unitarian," said Mom.

Grandma Flora crossed herself.

"They offer an excellent course for junior high students. It's called 'The Church across the Street.' They study a different religion each week, and the following Sunday, they go to that church for a service. Later, they can decide for themselves what to believe."

"Kathleen, look, I'm begging!" said Grandma. "T.R., when he's big, he chooses his own name. Danny, when he's grown, decides what religion he'll be. What's the point of parents, I ask you?"

"Flora . . ." Mom put out her hand and touched Grandma's arm. "There's only one parent now, and I'm doing the best I can. Don't make it more difficult for me."

"Believe me, I love you like a daughter! But why not a good Catholic? Why not a good Presbyterian? Baptist, even?"

"Because I like what Unitarians believe, that no one can be excommunicated except by the death of goodness in his own heart. To me, that's important."

"What's 'excommunicated'?" I asked Danny later. "Firing squad or hanging?"

Danny laughed. "It's when a church kicks you out."

"Oh."

I was even dumber than Grandma thought. I got a piece of paper and wrote down everything I knew about God to see just how smart or stupid I was:

1. He made the world.
2. Jesus is his little kid.
3. Jesus died.
4. Christmas is when he was born and Easter's when he died.

I wasn't entirely sure about that one but I kept going:

5. Adam and Eve were the first married people.
6. If you break one of the Commandments, you go to hell.

I wasn't sure about that one either, but I was running out of things to write. I stared at my list. That was it. That was everything I knew. I think there was some guy named Abraham in the Bible, but I'd forgotten what he did. If a madman ever put a gun to my head and said he'd kill me unless I told a Bible story, I'd have to make one up. It was that bad.

After dinner that evening, Grandma wanted to see the development, so she put on her orthopedic shoes and I took her for a walk. She liked the streets named after spices, especially Clove Terrace and Dill Drive, and I showed her where Mickey lived and told her about cow-pattie bingo.

We went to Curry Lane, too, just to see if Paul was shooting baskets. He was. Paul wants to be a professional player, and he spends hours out there practicing his hook shots, overhead drops, underhand lay-ups, and every time he tries a long shot, he stops first and makes a mark on the ground.

"You know what he's doing?" Grandma Flora said to me, as we watched him rise up slowly and lift the ball. "Making the sign of the cross."

"Does he thinks it helps?" I asked, as Paul thrust his arms forward and delivered.

Whump!

Grandma looked at me. "He made the basket, didn't he?" she said, and led me home triumphantly.

Lake Tarragon by Moonlight

Grandma Flora went to visit Aunt Celia for a few days after she left us, and she'd only been gone half an hour when Aunt Mavis called from Evanston. Danny was in the bathroom and Mom had gone to pick up the mail, so it was just Mave and me.

"T.R., we haven't heard from you yet, and wondered if everything was okay," she said. Aunt Mavis's frown lines travel along the telephone wires and crawl out the phone right into your ear. When I didn't answer in a tenth of a second, she said, "Well, is it?"

"Is what?"

"Okay. Is everything okay?"

"No."

"What's wrong?"

"Nothing. I just said things weren't okay. That doesn't mean there's anything wrong."

Silence. "T.R.," said Aunt Mavis, more slowly. "What is not okay?"

"Everything. Everything is new and shiny, the people are weird, and the only good thing is that if we become Unitarians, we can't be excommunicated."

"What in the world are you talking about?"

"Mom said if you called before she got back, I should make conversation."

"You are the limit!" Aunt Mavis was pretty angry. She makes me angry, and then I make her angry, and there are some people in the world that telephones just shouldn't connect.

This time the silence had a big fat sigh in the middle of it.

"T.R., aren't you and Danny making any friends?" she asked finally.

"That's hard to say, Aunt Mavis, because, like I said, the people here are weird. This guy . . . well . . . he hangs around basketball courts at night, you know? And this girl goes into toilets and tries to get guys to follow her."

"I knew it, *knew* it! I *knew* you were going to fall in with the wrong crowd!" Aunt Mavis said.

"Wait a minute, here's Mom," I told her, as the front door opened, and I hightailed it outside. Mom told me later that moving to Rosemary Acres might extend our lives some, but it certainly wasn't helping her sister.

I was sorry Grandma Flora was gone, because that meant that Danny and I were in charge of Mom again. It had been easier when we lived with Aunt Cis, because she and Mom had long talks in the evenings, and some-times Cis would invite people over that Mom might like to meet. But now Mom just had me and Danny and Rosemary Acres to keep her company. Danny never felt he should go anywhere until he knew that Mom had plans of her own for the day.

We hadn't even met our next-door neighbors yet. Once in a while, if the house was very quiet, we could hear a thump or footsteps on the other side of the wall. I looked out once and saw a man and woman leaving their house together. They both had on dark suits, and they both carried briefcases in their left hands. Danny thinks they're lawyers. I think they're morticians or something.

We were sitting out on the back steps once and Mom said, "What's that sweet smell? Is that clover?"

"Embalming fluid," I told her, but she didn't think it was funny.

Anyway, Danny did what he could for Mom. He helped hang all her pictures and put casters under the legs of the sofa. When he tried to put up her spice rack, though, he ran the drill straight through to the dining room, and Mom said maybe she didn't need her spice rack on the wall. Every so often he made a detour over to the bulletin board in the community center to see if there were any announcements of something Mom could do.

"What's this note about square dancing?" Mom said one day as she set some chicken salad on the table for lunch. "Did somebody call, Danny?"

"No, I just saw it on the bulletin board and thought you might be interested," Danny said.

Mom smiled and squeezed his shoulder as she passed his chair. "If I worked twenty-four hours a day from now until school begins, I couldn't do all the things I have waiting for me. But thanks, anyway."

Without Dad, though, Danny felt responsible for her. We were riding around with Paul later when Danny asked him how old his father was.

"Forty-eight going on eighty-four," said Paul, which wasn't very encouraging.

"What's he do?" asked Danny.

"His primary occupation is feeling sorry for himself, if you want to know," Paul told us.

If Danny was thinking about getting Mom and Mr. Bremmer together, I guess that killed it. I was glad, too, because I wasn't sure I'd like Paul for a stepbrother. I didn't know why exactly; Danny seemed to get along with him okay, but I never felt 100 percent comfortable with Paul.

He was too moody for one thing. Sometimes we'd ride over to pick him up, and he wouldn't smile once the whole afternoon. Other times he'd seem okay when we started out, and then zap! Just like that. Some little thing would tick him off. And sometimes he'd say something really mean—like there was so much anger inside him it sort of leaked out his mouth. He told me once I smelled like rotten armpits, and acted like he was going to throw up.

"Go change your socks, T.R.," was all Danny said, and for once I wished Danny could have said it a little differently.

But most of the time I got along okay with Paul, and when I didn't I just cleared out and left him with Danny. Danny gets along with everyone, but of course that's what worries Aunt Mave.

The next day we found a new list of rules from management in our mailbox. Mom taped it above the kitchen counter. I was gluing a model race car that had been broken during the move, and stood holding the parts together while I read:

Rules for Rosemary Acres

Rosemary Acres has been designed so that its appearance, both as individual townhouses and as a development, is aesthetically pleasing. For this reason, the exteriors of the units cannot be changed without approval.

1. Colors cannot be changed.
2. Beach towels, bedspreads, clothing, etc. cannot be hung on balconies and porches, or draped over railings.
3. Miniblinds must remain on all windows to present a unified appearance.
4. Nothing can be planted at the fronts or sides of townhouses without the prior approval of the landscaping committee.

I imagined a lone dandelion poking up through the dirt in front of somebody's door, and the landscaping squad leaping out of trucks to spray it dead. The list went on and on. Some of the rules were the same as the old ones, but I noticed that Miss Quinn had added, "No bicycles on lawns," "No skateboarding," and "No fireworks."

Paul Bremmer stopped by later to tell us he got new batteries for his boat, if we wanted to try it out.

"You see all these rules?" I asked him.

He nodded, and recited some of them by heart. Hours adults could swim in the pool, hours children could swim in the pool, what you could do at the lake (fish), what you could not do at the lake (boat and swim).

I was eating a banana with pretzel sticks stuck in it, then dipped in Hershey's chocolate syrup and frozen for twenty minutes. This is my own original recipe, but Paul didn't want any.

"Who do you suppose made up all those rules?" I asked.

"Quinn, who else?" he said, and went upstairs to get Danny.

When we got down to Lake Tarragon, Mickey was there in her cutoffs, and she was with her other brother this time—the stepbrother. He looked to be about a year or so younger than me, and he had on brand-new sneakers, white tube socks that came up to his knees, and a striped knit shirt with a white collar and matching shorts. He looked like one of those nerds in advertisements, with his hair combed, handing his mom a present on Mother's Day. Mickey probably couldn't do a thing about him because she got him along with her stepdad— a package deal.

Paul stopped there on the path, Danny bumping into

him from behind, and I knew it was because he felt embarrassed about playing with his boat in front of Mickey. That really teed me off because I'd been waiting all this time to try it out.

"Go on!" I said, furious that he might change his mind. "Hey, Mickey, want to see Paul's boat?"

"Sure," she said. She was squatting on the bank, poking a long stick in the water. Paul didn't have a choice.

"Hey, that's really neat!" the brother said in a high, whiny voice that'll get you somewhere with your mom, maybe, but nowhere with your friends. If the five of us started hanging around together, I hoped I wouldn't get stuck with him.

"So you're a boat captain now," Mickey said to Paul, holding back a smile. "Haven't I seen you somewhere before . . . like riding around in front of my house?"

Paul actually blushed. First time I'd seen him do that.

"Uh . . . Mickey . . . that's Paul Bremmer, and this is my brother, Danny," I said.

"Well, I'm trying to figure out why we can't swim in the lake," she said. "It doesn't seem very deep. The water only comes up to here." And she showed us on the stick.

"No swimming, no boating, no laughing, no breathing," said Paul.

"Maybe there are snakes in it," offered the brother.

"That's Norman," said Mickey. "One of my brothers."

"Stepbrother," Norman told us, which made him even more of a jerk.

"Gus, the baby, is my half brother," said Mickey.

"Which half?" asked Danny, and he and Paul and Mickey laughed.

You know what you do around girls when you're twelve? Laugh a lot. I'd sure seen a lot of teeth lately. But I still didn't want to be stuck with Norman. What we needed, I told myself, was a friend who was somewhere between my age and Danny's—somebody to sort of fill in the gaps, so that when Danny and Paul thought of me, they wouldn't lump me with Mickey's little brothers and count me out.

Paul turned his attention to the lake again. "There probably aren't any drop-offs," he said. "It's just scooped out with a bulldozer." He looked at Mickey. "How long have you lived here?"

"About a month longer than you. I watched you move in."

"No kidding?" Paul blushed again.

We fooled around by the water for a while. Paul let both me and Norman have a chance to control the boat, while Danny just sat there against a tree looking cool. I wished Mickey wasn't there. Paul and Danny would have played with the boat themselves if she wasn't. Now they just pretended they'd brought it down for me. So I let Norman have it all to himself, and practiced skipping stones on the water. I forget who taught me how to skip stones, Dad or Grandpa Gil.

When we all left, Nerdy Norman in the lead, I heard Danny, Paul and Mickey, behind me, making plans to sneak down to the lake some night and go swimming. And when I realized they meant *that* night, I knew I wouldn't be able to stand it if they didn't include me.

As soon as I was alone with Danny, I said, "You're not going out without me, are you?"

At first he pretended he didn't know what I was talking about.

"Swimming in the lake," I said.

"Well, sometime, maybe."

"Not sometime. Tonight. I heard." And then I added, "I'll just be your lookout."

I was glad I added that, because Danny said, "Okay, but don't tell Mom." As if I would.

The good thing about when you first move in someplace is that your mom's so busy she doesn't know where you are half the time. She might not even know you're gone. The bad thing about just moving in is you eat the same stuff every night. Cheese and crackers and tomato soup. Microwave pizza. Lean Cuisine. Everything said Stouffer's or Sara Lee on the box.

But wouldn't you know that for the first time since we'd come to Rosemary Acres, Mom asked what we were going to do that evening. Danny and I looked at each other.

"Tonight?" said Danny.

"There's a good program on public television. It's on Alaskan huskies. I think you'd like it."

"We're going over to Paul's. Maybe we'll watch it there," said Danny. I was really glad he said *we*.

Mom looked pleased. "I'm so glad you've found a friend."

We went over to Paul's street and shot baskets. Once it got dark, though, Paul reached under a bush, pulled out a towel, and the three of us walked down the path to Lake Tarragon, our swimming jams under our jeans. I felt like a faithful Saint Bernard, ready to yelp if anyone was coming. Ready to save Danny if he went under.

Everything looks different in the moonlight. The moon was almost full, so that Danny, walking down the path ahead of me, left a shadow. Fireflies flickered in the tall grass on either side.

"That's one thing you don't see in Oregon," Paul said. "Fireflies."

I never knew that. "That's where you're from?" I asked.

Paul nodded. "Dad was in the army, but now he has a civilian job," he said. And then, to Danny, "think she'll come?"

"She said she would."

We reached the bank and took off our jeans. I was afraid Danny would remind me I was only the lookout, but he didn't.

Paul was grinning. He nudged Danny. "Think she'll come in the buff?"

"What's that?" I asked.

"Jeez! Don't you know *any*thing?" Paul asked.

Danny, though, covered for me. "You know what it is, T.R. Skinny-dipping. In the raw."

"Oh, yeah," I said. "That's what I figured."

And then I thought about it. What if she *did* come in the buff? Boy, I didn't know if I was ready for this. "A girl's body is a temple to be revered and respected," it said in *From Boyhood to Manhood*. I was *sure* I wasn't ready for this.

The three of us waded in up to our knees, but we kept looking up the path toward the townhouses. The bottom of the lake felt squishy and slick.

"Primordial ooze," said Paul.

We sloshed around, letting our feet sink into the lake bottom, lifting each foot up one at a time. The mud made a sucking sound.

"I'll bet she doesn't come," said Danny at last. "I'll bet her mom found out and stopped her."

"Maybe she was just leading us on. Wants to keep us waiting down here," said Paul.

"Well, let's go swimming anyway," I said, but then we saw her. She was coming down the path in cutoffs and a tank top, and she didn't make a sound. The moonlight made the top of her hair all shimmery.

All three of us just stood there, knee-deep in the water, as Mickey unzipped her shorts. I knew I shouldn't be staring, but Danny and Paul were doing it, too. What if she didn't have anything on underneath? What if she just swam around in the water with her bottom bare? I felt like I was facing the River of Lust, but without my helmet, my boots, and my sword.

Mickey had on a bathing suit underneath.

"What did you tell your folks?" Danny asked, as Mickey leaned one hand against a tree and untied her sneakers.

"I didn't tell them anything. I climbed out a window."

Now we were really staring.

"The tool shed's just outside my room," said Mickey. "If they find out I'm gone, though, I'll get heck for sure. So I can't stay very long."

"How are you going to get back in?" Paul asked her.

"Same way. You'll have to give me a boost."

For the second time since we'd moved to Rosemary Acres, I decided I was in love with Mickey.

Paul said that the only safe thing to do was form a chain, and walk all along the lake bottom checking for holes and drop-offs. Nobody even thought of me as the lookout anymore. So with me about three feet from the bank, then Danny, then Mickey, and Paul farthest out, we all held hands, stretching our arms as far as they'd go, and walked slowly, beginning at the lower end of the lake. I felt like one of the early pioneers, exploring a lake that no one had charted before. I'll bet my fourth-grade teacher would have been pleased, especially if I stepped on something awful.

We kept going until we'd gone about halfway. We couldn't feel any big holes, just uneven places, and decided that was enough for one night—we'd swim, but only in the part of the lake we'd covered.

It's really weird to be out at night when your Mom thinks you're somewhere else, swimming in a lake you're not supposed to be in, with a girl in a green bathing suit that came up high on the sides. I think we all felt a little strange. We didn't talk a lot, and nobody did a lot of splashing, because we didn't want anyone to hear. When Danny and Paul did say something, it didn't sound much like them at all.

"All kinds of strange things are supposed to happen under a full moon," Paul said, squatting down in the water until just his head stuck out. He looked like a floating head.

"Like what? People go mad?" Mickey asked.

"Yeah. Dogs howl, and guys turn into werewolves," said Danny.

"Somewhere I heard that more women have babies when the moon is full. Something to do with gravity," Paul told us.

I wondered if I'd ever be able to say something like that to a girl. About having babies, when you're swimming at night in a lake. It was like we were all getting ready to spawn or something.

Then all at once Mickey got out, saying she'd better go home, and Paul and Danny were saying, yeah, they had to get home, too, and we were passing Paul's towel around, everyone using it, and I had it after Mickey. The same towel that had dried her legs was drying mine.

We all went single file back up the path through the tall grass, feeling very different, very grown-up. We stayed in the shadows when we got to the alley behind Coriander. Mickey had left the gate to her backyard open because it squeaked, so I stayed out in the alley as a lookout.

I watched while Paul and Danny crept through the tiny yard with Mickey. When they reached tool shed, they grasped each other's arms to make a platform and Mickey climbed up on it, a hand on each of their heads.

They boosted her onto the roof of the shed, and she crawled up the shingles toward her window.

Just then a light came on in the window, and there was Norman the Nerd.

"I'm gonna tell," he said.

The In-Between

Danny, Paul, and I stood out in the alley for a while after Mickey's light went out.

"I'll bet she's getting heck," said Paul.

I was furious at Norman. "That nerd!" I said. "That creep!"

Danny hunched his shoulders, hands in the pockets of his jeans. "They'll probably ground her for a year."

Our wet jams were soaking through our pants, so we said goodbye to Paul at the corner and went home to change. We made sure our hair was dry, then went looking for Mom. She was down in the family room, watching the program on Alaska, and sorting socks from the dryer.

"Can me and Danny have the rest of the ice cream?" I asked.

"May Danny and I," said Mom. "Yes, you may." The schoolteacher mom.

I got some bowls and divided the ice cream three

ways, then gave one to her, too. But all the while I was thinking what I'd say to Norman when I saw him again. Tattletale! Tattletale! Stick your head in a garbage pail!

"I don't know how huskies survive in all that cold," Mom said, savoring her ice cream. "And when food is scarce for families, what do the dogs eat?"

"They eat each other's poop," I said.

Mom and Danny looked at me.

"I read it somewhere," I told them. I didn't have a good thing to say about anyone, dogs included. I was that mad at Norman.

The phone rang, so I ran upstairs to answer. It was Mickey, only her voice sounded far away.

"T.R.?" she said.

"Yeah? Is that you, Mickey?"

"I can't talk very loud because I'm in the closet."

"They locked you in a closet?"

"No, I've got the phone in the closet. Just tell Danny it's okay. Norman didn't tell because I said if he did I'd tell Mom what he did on the Fourth of July, and that shut him up quick."

"What'd he do?" I asked.

"Peed in Gus's wading pool and Gus drank the water."

Double creep, I thought.

"So tell Danny to tell Paul, okay?" And she hung up.

I went down to the family room with a smirk on my face.

"Saved by a pee," I whispered to Danny.

"What?"

"Tell you later," I said.

"Isn't Alaska beautiful?" said Mom.

The next weekend we drove back into Chicago to have dinner at Aunt Celia's. As soon as I heard the noise of traffic, I felt homesick all over again—people and noise and laughter and sirens, always something going on somewhere, somebody to watch. Mom said we could go see our friends while we were there as long as we had a decent conversation with Cis first.

Aunt Celia was waiting, and threw her arms around us, one by one. She'll look just like Grandma Flora when she's old. Already she has a little bit of silver in her hair. Who she looks like most is Dad, though. Same straight nose, dark eyes, beautiful teeth. I bet she'll go on hugging us even after we're grown men whether we like it or not. I think I'll always like it; I don't know about Danny.

We sprawled in the wicker chairs on her porch, and she poured lemonade for everyone, then sat across from me.

"Dad sent balloons," I told her.

"He did? Well, wasn't that nice!" Aunt Cis glanced at Mother, but Mom didn't say anything, so Aunt Cis took another swallow of lemonade and held the glass against her cheek. "I miss you guys," she said.

"We miss you, too," I told her. "Miss being here . . ."

"But aren't you having any fun out in the country? All that open space?"

I didn't say anything. Danny didn't either. I felt sorry for Mom right then, but the truth was that the most fun we'd had so far was going down to the lake to swim, and nobody was supposed to know about that.

Aunt Cis lifted one bare foot and poked me with her toe. "Well, aren't you?"

"Some of the time," I said.

Celia had invited Keith for supper, too. Aunt Mavis and her husband were up in Milwaukee visiting Grandpa Gil, so we had Aunt Cis and Keith all to ourselves.

With Keith, I told the whole truth. When Mom and Cis went inside to cook, and he asked, "How's it going, guys?" I answered, "Homesick."

"I know what you mean," he said, and I was glad he didn't try to tell us we weren't. "When I first went to college at Northwestern, I didn't think I could ever miss Milwaukee. Chicago seemed to have everything. But that first night in the dorm—oh, boy."

"You missed Grandpa Gil?" asked Danny.

"Mom, too. She was alive then. It just hit me all of a sudden. Really surprised me. Kept thinking about all my friends, and figured I'd made one horrible mistake." Keith tipped back in his chair and put his feet on the railing. "I called Dad and told him I wanted to come home, and he said, 'Give it six weeks, Keith.' He was right. Took only a couple weeks, not six, but I was hardly ever homesick after that."

"What made the difference?" I asked.

"Friends. Family. Letters from home. You always carry your friends with you, know what I mean? Hey!" He grinned at Danny and me. "Did Dad bring any fireworks with him on the Fourth?"

We grinned back. "The only fireworks at Rosemary Acres, and all of them illegal," Danny said. Then we went inside the house to call all our old friends.

I'd been thinking we needed an "in-between" friend. Paul was thirteen, Danny and Mickey were twelve, and if we just had someone eleven, then ten wouldn't seem that much different. Our "in-between" moved there the following week, into the last remaining townhouse at Rosemary Acres—the one over on Parsley Place.

I was riding around on my bike when the van pulled up, so I sat watching the movers put down the ramp. They unloaded all the little stuff first, the kind they pack in at the end—folding chairs, a card table, a sled, a bike. . . .

It was a great bike—a trail bike, green and silver, with ten speeds. I wondered if the guy who owned it felt as bad about moving here as Danny and I did. Then he came out of the house to get his bike, and I saw that he was a little taller than me, shorter than Danny. Brown skin, black hair, black eyes. He just had to be eleven.

"Hi," I called.

He looked over at me, but didn't smile. "Hi," he said.

Maybe he already had friends. Maybe every weekend a dozen relatives came to visit and he wouldn't need any new friends at all.

"Nice bike," I called after him.

He stopped then, and pretended he was wiping something off the back fender, so I rode over.

"I got it for my birthday," he said.

"Which birthday?"

"Eleventh."

Bingo!

"Any place around here to ride?" he asked.

"Pepper Road, Basil Boulevard, Cinnamon Court, and every other spice you can think of." I grinned.

He smiled a little, too.

"I'm T.R. I live over on Cajun Drive," I told him.

"What's the T.R. mean?"

"Nothing. Those are my Dad's initials."

The boy just studied me. Then, "I'm Randall," he said.

A little girl, maybe three, came out of the house, followed by her mother.

"That's Leah," Randall said. "She my sister."

"*She's* my sister," his mother said.

Oh boy, I thought, another schoolteacher mom.

But Randall grinned. "No, she's not. She's *my* sister," he said, and his mother laughed.

"We're the Hayes family," she told me.

"We're the Scarlinos," I told her. "We almost bought this house."

I saw Mrs. Hayes stiffen. "What's wrong with it?"

"Nothing. Actually, we liked it better. Danny and I didn't like the name of the street, that's all."

Mrs. Hayes looked at me curiously, then smiled.

What I hoped was that Randall would invite me up to his room, but he didn't. I sat on my bike and watched while he went in and out, but finally he dropped a whole box of Legos, and when I offered to help pick it up, he said sure. After that it was easy. I knew how to keep out of the movers' way, and pretty soon even his parents started handing me things to take in.

Randall had a lot of great things: a globe that was rough on the surface, showing the mountains; a guinea pig named Susie; a collection of sharks' teeth; a zillion comic books; and a whole bunch of boxes that he just called "my equipment."

"*What* equipment?" I asked after we'd carried up still another one. I peeked inside. It looked like junk.

"Just stuff, man! Just stuff."

Randall's dad brought up some root beer later. "Sorry we don't have anything to eat, but it's going to be McDonald's for a few nights until we're settled in," he said. "Don't even have a place to sit, hardly."

He was a big man—tall and heavy, but not fat. He looked like he could have been a football player, but Randall said he was a life-insurance salesman.

"That's okay," I said, taking one of the root beers. "The day we moved in, we ate on the floor."

"Good idea," said Randall, and sat down with his back against the wall. I sat down beside him, and as the two of us were enjoying our pop, I realized that Leah was getting the room with the racing-car wallpaper, and Randall had the room that Danny was going to get if we'd taken this house instead. I started to grin.

"What you grinning at?"

I pointed. "See that window over there?"

"Yeah?"

"If there was a woman in that house taking off her

clothes, you could turn out your lights and watch."

Randall looked at me. "You're weird, man."

"It was my brother's idea," I told him, embarrassed.

"How many brothers you got?"

"Just one. You have any?"

"Nope. Only Leah."

"Well, you can hang out with us if you want to. We've got this friend named Paul. He's a basketball player. You shoot baskets?"

"Naw."

"What do you like to do?"

"Stuff," Randall told me, and nodded toward his boxes in the corner.

If Aunt Mavis was still worried about us, I was pretty sure she'd like Randall. She'd like Mickey and Norman, too. If Aunt Mave was going to worry about anyone, I decided, she should worry about Paul. He's the one we'd known here longest and, at the same time, the one we knew least.

Hanging Out

The next morning when I got up, I couldn't find either Mom or Danny, but I heard noises from in front of the house. Mom was sitting on the curb with an open book in her lap, and Danny was tinkering around under the hood of the Chevy. I made myself some toast and took it outside.

The book in Mom's lap was *The Woman's Auto Handbook.* "Uh oh," I said under my breath. The only person in our family who knew anything about cars was Dad.

"What's wrong with it?" I asked.

"Nothing. But I bought this book to help me keep up on maintenance, and there's a checklist of things to do," Mom said. And then, to Danny, "Did you find the dipstick?"

Danny nodded. "Oil's one quart low, Mom," he said, looking hard at a metal stick. "I think," he added, but not loud enough for Mom to hear.

"I'll add some the next time I go to the service

station," Mom said. "What about the radiator?"

"You've got plenty of water, but there's crud all over your battery."

"Oh no! Now what?" Mom got up and both of us looked under the hood. There was white lava caked on top of the battery. Mom looked up "battery" in the index and began to read: "Grease and acid can form on the terminal leads of your battery and interfere with electrical contact. Use a toothbrush and clean them with clear ammonia or a solution of baking soda and water . . ."

"Don't use my toothbrush," I said, taking another bite of toast.

"When the bubbling action occurs," Mom read on, "wipe away with a rag. Do *not* get acid on hands. Do *not* handle the battery with the engine running. Do *not* . . ."

I went back inside to finish my breakfast and took the Yellow Pages to the table with me. I looked up both "mechanics" and "hospitals," ready to dial whichever we'd need first.

We didn't, though. By the time I finished my third bowl of Clusters and ate a banana, the battery was cleaned and Danny was checking the tires.

"T.R.," Mom said coming back in the kitchen. "Do you have a dime? I've only get nickels and quarters, and so does Danny."

I went up in my room to check, but had mostly pennies.

"This is ridiculous!" said Mom. "The book says I should take a dime and insert it top-side down into a groove in my tires; if I can see the top of Roosevelt's head, then I need new tires—but I can't find a dime!"

"I'll get one from Randall," I said, needing an excuse to get away.

This time I took the alley behind Parsley Place because it's closer. I opened the Hayes's back gate and was going up the stone walk to the house when I heard a voice say, "Hey, dude!"

I stopped and looked around, but the yard was empty.

"Hey, *dude!*" the voice said again, and seemed to be coming from under a bench on the patio. I stared.

"Hey, Texas Ranger, up here!"

I looked up and saw Randall grinning at me from his window. He was holding a microphone in his hand, and then I saw the wire that came down the side of the house, attached to a tiny speaker under the bench. I laughed.

"Come on up," he said. "The door's open."

Up in Randall's room, I saw his stuff spread out all over the bed—all kinds of junk, a lot of electronic gadgets.

"What I want to do, see, is figure out a way you can talk to me from outside when I'm up in my room. I have these two old cassette players, and I took out their microphones. I'm going to put the second one outside."

"Neat!" I said. I didn't say, of course, that if I wanted to talk to him, I could use the telephone. Or that if I was down here and he was up in his room he could just open his window. That wasn't the point. The point was to figure out something that would make this house different from any other blue-shuttered townhouse on the street.

"What I need," he said, "is more wire." He looked at me. "What you going to do today, Texas Ranger?"

"What's with the Texas Ranger bit?"

"T.R.," he said. "You've got to be something."

I grinned. "Well, I came to borrow a dime, for one thing. Mom needs it. You have any?"

Randall looked in his drawer and found one for us.

"We usually shoot baskets with Paul Bremmer in the mornings," I told him. "Sometimes we swim in the pool. Want to come?"

"Naw. Be working on this. You come back later, maybe I'll have it done."

Mom's tires were fine, so Danny and I went up to the pool about eleven. Mickey was there with Gus the Gross and Norman the Nerd. Gus was sitting in the kiddie pool, chewing his rubber boat with one hand and splashing water with the other, and Norm was walking on the sides of his feet, howling because the concrete was too hot. I think Mickey got all the good genes in that family and the defective ones went to Gus and Norman.

"Listen," Mickey said when she saw Danny. "You want to go to the mall this afternoon?"

"There's a mall?"

"About a mile west of here. I usually walk it. Mom lets me go as long as I'm with someone and I stay off the highway."

"Sure," said Danny. "I'll see if Paul wants to go."

I could hardly stand it, waiting for someone to include me. Then Mickey said, "The only catch is I've got to take Norman. Mom wants him out of her hair today."

I didn't even wait for an invitation. "I've got this neat friend who just moved in," I said. "Could I ask him?"

And Mickey was real nice about it. "Whoever wants to go," she said. "Come over around two, okay?"

Paul said he'd go, but at two he still hadn't come, so Danny and I set off for his place. When we got to his house, Paul was in the doorway, his back to us, so we just waited out on the sidewalk. He must have been talking to someone, because he started to edge out the door, then stopped, then went inside again, then got halfway out and stopped. We could hear voices arguing, but we couldn't make out what they were saying.

Finally Paul wheeled around and came down the steps, leaving the door open, and someone closed it after him. He didn't even say hi when he saw us. He just charged on down the street so we had to hustle to keep up.

I realized that while Paul had been in our house a lot of times—eaten with us, in fact—he'd never once invited us inside his. I wondered what his dad was like. Other than feeling sorry for himself, I mean.

After a block, though, Paul began to slow down. Danny seemed to know how to handle Paul; he just waited him out. "Where to?" Paul asked, like he just noticed we were there.

"Pick up Mickey and Norman, then swing over to Parsley Place and get this new friend of T.R.'s," Danny said.

When we reached Coriander, Mickey and Norman were waiting out front, and then we all set off for Randall's. Norm was wearing a lime-green T-shirt, with pink and lime checked shorts. I could hardly stand to look at him.

Paul calmed down a lot once Mickey was with us. It almost seemed as though he got along better with girls than he did with Danny and me sometimes. We got to the house on Parsley, and when Randall came to the door, I introduced him to the others.

"You want to hang out at the mall with us?" Mickey asked him. "It's about a mile up the road. We're going to walk."

We could see Randall's father in the hallway behind him, listening, and then he came to the door. He had on a suit and tie this time, like he was just about ready to go out. He was smiling at Mickey, but he directed his questions to me.

"What's that mean, 'hang out'? What are you going to *do*?"

I looked at Danny. How did you describe hanging out?

Danny shrugged. "Look around," he said.

"It's like this," Mr. Hayes said. "You've got something to do, something to buy, some reason for going, Randall can go. You just going to stand around, see what's happening, he can't." Randall was examining one elbow, head down.

"We need some wire," I said quickly.

Randall started to smile.

"Okay, he can go. You all go get your wire, have a pop

or something, ride the escalators, check out the theaters, and come on home," Mr. Hayes said. Then he looked at Randall. "But don't you be waiting around for something to happen. Got it?"

"Okay," Randall said. He went back upstairs for some money, and then we started off.

"Wow!" said Mickey. "Your dad must have gone to the same school with my mom, and they both had the same teacher. That's just what she always says."

The air was hot. We started out in a ditch along the highway, but then the land leveled off, and the fence on our right began to swing in a little. There was a worn path as far as we could see. Cars and trucks zoomed by to the left of us, but we felt safe over in the weeds. I sniffed again for clover. I wanted to be able to tell Mom I'd smelled some. We finally reached a little corner of woods where we walked in shade for about a quarter of a mile.

I knew that Danny and Randall were going to get along, and Randall and Mickey, but I wasn't so sure about Paul. Danny was telling Randall about the fireworks on our lawn on the Fourth of July, and Mickey told him about cow-pattie bingo. Randall smiled real wide, and I knew he was enjoying himself. But Paul hardly said a word.

There was a breeze in the woods, and it felt good after the long walk in the heat. When we came out on the other side, though, the sun hit us full in the face, and Norm really howled.

"It's too hot!" he yelped, stopping like he wasn't going on.

"It's not much farther," Mickey told him. "C'mon, Norm."

"I can't! I'll get a headache!" Norman cried.

"Well, why don't you sit here in the shade and wait till we come back," I suggested.

Norman really bellowed then. "No! I wanna stay with you!"

"Then move your feet, dude, not your mouth," said Randall.

Norman started walking, Paul started to smile, and I knew that Randall had just made the team.

Lytton's Corner wasn't a huge mall. Just two floors, escalators at both ends, a court in the middle with trees that almost reached the skylight, and lots of benches. There were three movie theaters, a Mrs. Fields cookie shop, Fannie May candy, McDonald's, an ice-cream parlor, plus clothing stores and a Radio Shack.

Randall headed straight for Radio Shack and found what he wanted. Paul needed new laces for his basketball shoes, and Norman wanted ice cream. We all got cones and sat outside the store to eat them.

"Trade you a bite of pistachio for one of double fudge?" Mickey asked Danny.

He grinned and held out his cone. She took a bite of his ice cream. Then he put his fingers around her cone—right over her hand—and took a bite of pistachio.

I held out my cone. "Want a bite of strawberry, Mickey?" I asked hopefully.

"No, thanks," she said. "I'm allergic to strawberries." I guessed it was going to be that kind of a day.

The six of us sat eating our ice cream, swinging our feet.

"You like Rosemary Acres?" Paul asked Randall.

Randall shrugged, took another bite. "Haven't hardly seen it yet. It's not like home, though."

"Where's home?"

"Indiana. We had a big house and a yard back there."

"How come you moved here, then?" Mickey asked.

"Dad got transferred."

It seemed as though all the people at Rosemary Acres—all *our* families, anyway—were there because of a change in their lives. Something had happened. Mom and Dad got a divorce; Mickey's mom had Gus; Paul's dad left the army; Randall's dad got a transfer. In a way, our families were hanging out—waiting to see what would happen.

I glanced over at Paul. He wasn't looking at Randall anymore. He wasn't even looking at Mickey. He was studying a man and a boy outside a shoe store, probably father and son. They were talking together, laughing about something, kidding around. Paul watched with his lips slightly apart, his eyes fixed. The ice cream dripped on his hand, and Paul blinked. He stared down at his cone, then walked over and dropped it in a trash can. The whole cone!

"Let's go," he said suddenly, standing up. I looked at Danny. He just shrugged, and we all set off, following Paul down the escalator.

More about Paul

When I really began to worry about Paul Bremmer was after we got home—*long* after we got home. Randall and Mickey and I went to the pool to swim, and later, I was upstairs changing T-shirts when Danny came to the door of my room.

"You won't tell anyone, will you?" he said.

I looked over. "About what?"

"Paul."

"What about him?"

"You didn't see?"

Now I was really curious. "See what?"

Danny looked confused. "Never mind." He started across the hall to his own room, but I wouldn't let him go.

"What, Danny?" I said, grabbing his arm. "Tell me!"

"Never mind, I said!" Danny shook me loose and started to close his door, but I had one leg inside.

"If you don't tell me, I won't tell you where else

Mickey has freckles," I said.

Now it was Danny's turn to be curious. "You're bluffing."

"No, I'm not."

Danny sat down on the edge of his bed and began bouncing a small rubber ball against the floor. "I thought you saw Paul slip an extra pair of shoelaces in his pocket back at the store."

"He didn't pay for them?"

"No. Only the one pair."

"Why didn't you say anything?"

"I did, after we got back."

"What'd you say?"

"That I didn't think he'd stoop to something like that. He said he was just pissed off at the clerk for giving him all his change in pennies. Anyway, he said he'd put them back on the counter the next time we went to the mall."

"Yeah, I'll just bet he will. I wonder how much more he takes," I said.

Danny's eyes were on me, though. "Okay, where else does Mickey have freckles?"

"She has them on her back. I noticed them at the pool."

Danny stopped bouncing the ball. "For crying out loud, I knew that!"

"So? I didn't say any special place, did I?"

Danny threw the ball against his dresser and let it roll under his bed. "Go soak your head, T.R."

I left, but at least I'd found out something more about Paul. It made me feel worse, though, and I sure as heck couldn't tell Mom or Aunt Cis.

Later that afternoon, we went over to Paul's street to shoot baskets, and that seemed to be what Paul needed: a way to let off steam. I hadn't had much practice at basketball. In Chicago, we played street hockey in the evenings; it was the older guys who monopolized the one basket down the alley. But for Paul, basketball was serious. So mostly I just dribbled the ball around and threw it to Paul so he could practice turning and passing and rebounds.

Danny and I would take a rest once in a while, but not Paul. While we sat on the curb he'd keep right on practicing, and whenever he tried a really long shot, he'd always bend over first and make the sign of the cross on the pavement with the ball. Danny and I were always quiet when he did that. I mean, when you're religious ignoramuses, you don't know whether to bow your head or what. If he didn't make the basket after that, we never said anything, but he usually made it.

I wished I had a good-luck sign of some kind to make before I tried a long shot, because I always missed. I even missed a lot when I was standing near the basket.

"Take your time, T.R.," Paul said. "You're throwing a little too short. Keep your eye on the front of the rim and give a little extra push this time."

Paul and Danny waited off to the side to give me a chance to practice. I rubbed one arm over my forehead to wipe the sweat, and then suddenly I bent over and made a quick design on the concrete with the ball. I rose up real slow, the way Paul does, focused on the front of the rim, then flicked the wrist of my shooting hand toward the basket and rolled the ball off my fingertips, the way Paul said to do. It hit the rim and teetered a second or so, then slid through the net.

"Way to go, T.R.!" Danny said, as Paul retrieved the ball, and we began passing it back and forth again.

Even though we only had one backboard and net, Paul wanted to make everything as regulation as possible, so he went in his house and came back with a yardstick and chalk. He measured, and drew the end line, then the free-throw lane, then the circle at the end of it, and the free-throw line. He backed down the road and drew the halfway line across it, and had just started on the center circle when we noticed a car coming slowly down Curry Lane. When it got closer, we saw Miss Quinn, out making her daily rounds to be sure nobody had painted their shutters any color other than blue or planted any illegal flowers. She shook her head and tapped the horn to get Paul's attention.

Paul straightened up and looked at her. "What?"

"We really don't want to encourage that," she said, leaning out the window.

"Basketball?"

"Drawing on public property."

"But there's a basket and no court," Paul said, staring.

"Well, I guess the basket will have to do for now."

"But this is chalk!" put in Danny.

"We like things to look new," Miss Quinn went on.

"It's chalk!" Paul repeated. "It'll wash off in a couple rains."

Miss Quinn turned the car around. "We're particular,"

she said, and headed back toward Basil Boulevard.

"I don't believe it!" said Danny.

Paul whirled suddenly and started beating the ball against the concrete, harder and harder. *Wham, wham, wham,* back and forth under the basket. *Wham! Wham! Wham!* Like the ball was the enemy.

Whup! A hook shot, into the net. More whamming. Whup! A jump shot, into the net. Paul reminded me of one of the rockets Grandpa set off on the Fourth of July—propped up there on the grass, the fuse lit—just quivering and quivering. It seemed to sit there half a minute, then suddenly, ka-*blam!*

"Like a firecracker waiting to explode," I told Danny later as we walked home.

"Oh, he just gets that way," Danny said. "He stores up a lot of stuff."

"Yeah, he gets mad at a clerk so he steals shoelaces," I said. "He gets mad at Miss Quinn so he takes it out on the ball. What'll he do if he ever gets mad at you, Danny? Break your nose? Why do you want to go around with someone like that, someone who's always got a mad on?"

"Maybe he's got things to be mad about."

"That's just an excuse. Everybody has things to be mad about."

"You want me to give up on him just because he gets angry? You want me to give up on you when you do something dumb?"

Of course I didn't. And the fact was that no matter who Danny went around with, or what Danny did, I couldn't give up on *him* ever. I had to look out for him even more. Man, that was getting hard to do, though. I had to be the watchdog who never sleeps.

We switched to the side of the street where the houses shaded the walk, and then Danny focused on me. "What was that you drew on the concrete with the ball, T.R.?"

I was embarrassed. "Just something," I muttered.

"C'mon, you can tell me. Something religious?"

"How would I know religious?"

"That's what I'm asking."

I stared straight ahead. "A good-luck sign."

"What?"

I kept walking. "The hood ornament on Dad's car."

Danny stopped, but I kept going so he caught up with me. "A hood ornament?"

"I made the basket, didn't I?" I said.

Mom was out shopping, and we were glad, because there hadn't been anything much to eat in the house except pancake mix, canned tuna, eggs, and cereal for the last day and a half.

Boys, read a note on the refrigerator, *if you can't hold out until supper, open some tuna. Do not make pancakes!*

We'd made pancakes for breakfast, and because we were out of butter, we'd smeared them with marshmallow sauce before we poured on the syrup. Danny decided to hold out till supper, but I was eating a handful of dry cereal when the phone rang. It was Aunt Mavis.

"T.R., how are things going?" she asked. "Kathy said

she'd call me yesterday, but she didn't."

"She's in the hospital," I said. I don't know why I said that. Mom's younger sister just makes me say things I never meant to because she gets upset so easily. If Paul is a firecracker waiting to go off, Aunt Mavis is Old Faithful.

"What? What happened?" Now her voice was an octave higher, and before I could even think, she screeched, "T.R., tell me!"

"She's at the store," I said.

There was complete silence at the other end of the line. I imagined Aunt Mavis standing there with her eyes like two fried eggs.

"Why do you do things like this?" she asked finally.

"I don't know," I said. "I just do sometimes."

"Put Danny on," she commanded, so I did.

Taking the Wheat Chex upstairs, I sat by my window, looking out at the one tree the bulldozers forgot. I wondered if Mom had any idea how strange this place was to Danny and me, or how much we missed sitting out on the porch with Aunt Cis in the evenings—Aunt Cis and Mom and any of our friends who happened to pass by the house. I wondered if she remembered how much fun we'd had playing kick-the-can out in the dark while the grown-ups sat on the porch and talked. I thought about all the street noises, the lights going on and off in houses all up and down the block, and the breeze that blew in from the direction of the lake at a certain time each evening.

I was homesick for everything. The smell of the hot pavement after a rain; of a car that has driven twenty miles on the Outer Drive and is cooling down by the curb, the frame giving off little ticking noises; of the onion and garlic cooking in the house across the street. I missed the squeak of the porch swing, the clink of ice in a glass, the dips and swells from an accordion a few doors down. If I ever get married, I want a wife who cooks onions and garlic and plays the accordion.

Was this how the pioneers felt when they left their homes in the East and headed for Kansas? When they got there, did they look around and feel this big fat zero inside them—nothing to see but grass and trees? Out here at Rosemary Acres, we didn't even have trees.

At Rosemary Acres, all the houses are lined up like soldiers at inspection. They all have hedges that look like they've been trimmed by a U.S. Marines barber.

I was more worried about Danny and Paul than I'd realized. I imagined Paul stealing something else, something bigger, and Danny being arrested along with him, just because he was there. And then Mom and Aunt Cis and Aunt Mavis would ask me why I hadn't said something sooner, when I knew that Paul was into shoelaces.

I wanted to go downstairs and tell Mom when she got back, but I thought how she'd probably walk right up to Paul the next time he came over and say, "Paul, I know about your shoplifting habits, and I'll feel a lot better if you take those shoelaces back."

She's like that. Back in Chicago, we were going to try a new pediatrician, and some kid told me that he was a sadist who kept a jar of kids' eyeballs in his office. I told Mom, and when we got to the office, she said, "T.R.

heard that you keep a jar of eyeballs in here, Dr. Feld-man, and I wonder if you could reassure him." It turned out the jar had a bunch of glass marbles in it, and when I got to school the next day I pasted the kid in the mouth.

If I had a dad—one who was around, I mean—I'd go straight to him, but I couldn't see myself calling the University of California at Berkeley and telling Dad that maybe Danny was going to be arrested and maybe he wasn't. I decided I'd stick by Danny wherever he went anymore, not let him out of sight for a minute—not until we started school, anyway, and he started making other friends. If I saw Paul shoplift anything else, I'd sound the alarm right away. I'd yell at the top of my lungs so the store detectives would know that Danny and I weren't in on it.

We helped Mom put the groceries away when she got home, and after dinner, when she was talking to Aunt Cis on the phone, I saw Danny walk to the front door and stand there with his hands in his pockets.

"What are you doing, Danny?" I asked.

"Climbing Mount Everest," he said.

"Well, what are you thinking about doing?" I asked. "Going over to Paul's?"

"Maybe."

"Can I come?"

"Not tonight."

I had to stay cool. "Okay," I said, and went into the living room. I pretended I was reading a book, but I was listening for every little sound. Danny came back through on his way to the kitchen again. He stopped and stared at me.

"What's the matter?" I said. "Can't a guy read a book?"

"*Man's Archaeological Past?*" he said. And I realized I hadn't even noticed what I'd picked up.

"I like the photographs," I told him.

It was about eight-thirty when I heard the back screen close softly. I ran to the kitchen and waited just inside the door in the dark, listening to the sound of Danny's bicycle being wheeled around the corner of the house, then to the squeak of the back gate as it opened. I waited five seconds longer, then sneaked out the back door, grabbed my own bike, and went around to the alley. When I got to the end, I could just see Danny beneath the street light, turning up Curry Lane.

I was hiding behind a forsythia bush a few doors down from the Bremmers' when Paul came out of his house, and he and Danny set out on foot. I rammed my bike into the branches of the forsythia, waited until they had passed, then followed a half block behind.

They turned onto Basil and went past Cajun to Coriander where they turned again. They walked real slow when they passed Mickey's house, followed Coriander to where it crossed Ginger, then turned and came back. This time they walked back and forth in front of her house a few more times before they went on. What I couldn't figure was why, if they wanted to see Mickey, they didn't go to her door and knock? Call her on the phone? Why did they just keep hoping that if they hung around long enough, she'd drop into their laps?

This was a dumb idea, I decided. I followed them back out to Basil, but this time, instead of going back up to Paul's, they crossed the boulevard and went down the sloping hill toward the lake. My heart pounded a little harder. When I was sure they were halfway down the path, I crossed Basil, too, and started down, inch by inch. It was really dark in that tall grass. Once I stopped, certain that Paul was waiting for me in the weeds just ahead, then I heard voices farther on and kept going.

I stopped just before I got to the bank. I still couldn't figure out what they were saying, though, so I moved closer, trying not to make a sound, squatting down in the weeds at one side of the path.

"Really?" I heard Danny say.

"You dare me?"

There was a murmur. I strained to hear.

"I don't know." Danny's voice.

"Why not?"

"Maybe we ought to get T.R."

"Why? C'mon." Paul again.

And suddenly there was a flash, then a loud bang, then footsteps pounding on the path beside me.

A Burning Fuse

I crawled through the grass, my heart in my mouth. What I found, though, in the little bit of moonlight that filtered through the clouds, was just a scorched place there on the bank, the remains of a Fourth of July rocket, and a tin can not too far away. I could smell firecracker smoke.

Standing up, I disgustedly kicked the can back into the weeds as far as I could. Then I went back up the path to Basil Boulevard, walked to Curry Lane, and over to the forsythia bush where I'd hidden my bike. The bike was gone.

I went sort of crazy. I kicked the bush. I kicked the fence. I kicked every little tree I came to on Basil Boulevard, and they'll probably all grow up deformed. Clomping up the stairs at home, I almost dared someone to ask me where I'd been, but Mom was in her room writing letters and listening to the stereo, and Danny wasn't back yet. I threw myself on my bed and stared up into the dark.

Man, I hated Rosemary Acres almost more than anything else I could think of. Hated that I had to be Danny's watchdog. Hated that he and Paul had gone down to the lake to set off the rocket without me. Hated the fact that you couldn't leave your bike for a few lousy minutes without somebody stealing it. Right at that moment I knew what it felt like to be a dog after he risked his life, practically, to save somebody, and he wasn't even needed. When the somebody didn't even know he was there.

Danny came home about a half hour later, and I guess he saw me lying on my bed in the dark. He stuck his head through the doorway.

"T.R.?" he said.

At first I didn't answer. Finally I said, "Yeah?"

"What are you doing here in the dark?"

"Who cares?" I snarled.

Danny came on inside. "Hey, what's the matter?"

"You don't care!" I said.

"What do you mean I don't? What did I do?"

"You and Paul went down to the lake without me and set off a rocket in a can, and now my bike's gone." I decided I was more mad right then about my bike. I'd had it less than a year. Grandpa Gil had given it to me last Christmas, and it was gone already.

"Your bike's at Paul's," Danny said. "We saw it in a bush on our way back to his place, so we took it there. You can get it tomorrow." He studied me. "How did you know we set off that rocket?"

"Because I followed you down there. Because I'm

worried about you. Paul's weird and he steals things, and you keep on running around with him."

Danny was looking at me. I couldn't see his eyes in the dark, but you can tell by the way someone holds his head that he's looking right at you.

"All he took was a pair of shoelaces, T.R., and he's going to give them back."

"How do you know that's all he steals? Next thing we know *you'll* be taking stuff and saying it's only a pair of shoelaces." I was getting madder by the minute. "We've never been in Paul's house. We've never even met his father. How do you know they don't run a burglary ring and have a houseful of stolen stuff?"

"I don't," said Danny, and that shut me up. "You never know everything for sure, T.R. Some things you just have to trust."

"I wouldn't trust Paul Bremmer with anything," I said. "He's strange, he's always mad about something, you never know what he's thinking, and the least little thing sets him off. He's just the kind of person Aunt Mavis warned us about." I didn't think I'd ever find myself on the same side of the fence as Aunt Mavis, but there I was.

Danny was quiet a moment. Then he said, "His mom died, you know."

"No, I didn't know. How would I know unless someone tells me?"

"I don't know when it was, but his dad wanted to leave Oregon because there were too many memories. That's why he took a job here."

I couldn't understand. "So? I'd be sad, not mad."

Danny sat down on the edge of my bed. "What Paul's mad about is that his dad's all wrapped up inside himself, and it's like Paul lost both his parents. I guess he expected his dad to be there for him, and that's just never happened."

It sounds dumb, I know, but I'd forgotten that parents don't just divorce; sometimes they die. Then I felt rotten.

"I'm a jerk, Danny."

"No, you're not."

"I'm mouse dirt."

"Cut it out, T.R."

We were both quiet awhile. Then I asked, "What would you do, Danny, if Paul did get in big trouble some time? I mean, if he stole something really big and the police were after him and everything?"

"I don't know. Haven't even thought about it."

"If Paul ever got in big trouble and you were with him, you could go to jail too, Danny."

"Man, you *are* a worry wart."

"It could happen."

Danny punched me on the arm. "If I ever went to jail, you'd go in my room and take all my baseball cards, I'll bet."

"I would not!"

"My CDs."

"Don't be dumb."

"Yeah?" Danny was laughing. "If I went to jail tomorrow, what's the first thing you'd do?"

I thought about it. If Danny went to jail, *I'd* be Man of the House and have to know about cars.

"Learn where the dipstick goes," I said.

Danny laughed again. "G'night, Worry Wart."

"'Night, Danny."

After he left the room, I was thinking two things: First, that I'd have to know about a lot more than dipsticks; and two, that Danny always seems to be there for me when I need him, but who's always there for Danny? You can never seem to reach Uncle Keith at college; Uncle Lyle hardly says a word; and Grandpa Gil's nice, but he's old. Who could Danny really call if he needed to talk to a man? All he's got is some phone number out in California, that's it.

Every day, Randall had a new name for me.

"Hey, Trade Route," he said the next day when I returned the dime Mom borrowed. "Help me string up this wire."

What we had so far was a mike in his room and a speaker under the bench on the patio. What we needed was a mike on the patio and a speaker in his room.

"I don't know," I said. "What if I come by some night to leave a message, you're not in your room, I start jabbering away, and your mom hears everything?"

Randall thought that over. "I'll figure out something," he said.

We fooled around some more.

"You know what the worst thing is about a project like this?" Randall asked me.

"The wires get messed up?" I guessed, working to untangle the speaker wire that we had just dangled out the window.

"Nope. That you're always sorry when it's over. Then you have to think up something else to do."

I was thinking how General Electric would be glad to hire Randall some day. AT&T, maybe.

"I've got a good project for you," I said. "De-nerd Norman."

Randall laughed. "Those shorts got to go."

"And the tube socks up to his knees," I said.

"His whine."

"The way he scrunches up his face."

"You get rid of all that, not much going to be left of Norman," said Randall.

We took a break for lunch. Randall's dad was fixing BLTs, and he fried the bacon crisp, the way I like it. Leah was sitting across from us, swinging her legs under the table.

"Where's your mom?" I asked.

"Work," Randall said.

"She teach summer school?"

Randall stared at me. "She doesn't teach; she's a secretary, part-time."

I don't know what it is about mothers, but they all seem like teachers to me.

Danny and I finally got a chance to see inside Paul's house. Usually he was waiting outside when we went over, or shooting baskets at the end of his street. But on

Saturday, when we were taking his boat to the lake again, we'd got halfway down his walk when Paul remembered the batteries were back in his room. "C'mon up," he said.

Mr. Bremmer was sitting at the dining-room table when we came in, paper and notebooks spread out around him. He was a little bald, and was wearing a T-shirt over what looked like old army pants.

"Danny and T.R., Dad," Paul said as we traipsed through the dining room to the stairs at the back. In our house, the stairs are just inside the front door, but the Bremmers' townhouse was different because it was smaller.

His dad peered at us over his glasses, said hello without smiling, and went back to his work.

"What does he do?" Danny asked as we went upstairs.

"Accounting. Budgets and stuff."

There were only two bedrooms on the top floor of the Bremmers' house instead of three, and Paul led us to his at the back.

We got to the doorway and stared, because one whole wall in Paul's bedroom had been painted stoplight red. Another wall was brilliant blue, another green, and the fourth one was yellow. Bright yellow. You walk in Paul Bremmer's room, you think you've been trapped in a Crayola box.

"Yikes!" I said. "Did you do this yourself?"

Paul grinned a little. "You think anyone else would have painted it this way? Dad said I could decorate any way I wanted." Then he added, "I figured we needed *some*thing cheerful around here."

We stepped inside.

"Miss Quinn would have a cow!" said Danny, and we laughed.

Paul found the batteries and we went quietly back through the dining room. This time his father didn't even look up. I felt a little sorry for Mr. Bremmer right then, like maybe he had a right to be sad for a while. I guess when you're sad yourself, it's hard to remember that someone else is hurting, but arguing with him, the way Paul did, wouldn't help.

"Place is like a morgue," Paul said when we were back outside, and I figured Mr. Bremmer wasn't the only one feeling sorry for himself. I tried to think of something cheerful.

"Let's invite Randall to go with us," I said suddenly.

So we went up the alley behind Parsley Place, opened the gate, and I showed them the mike under the bench on the patio. This time, though, there was something new, something that looked a little like a mousetrap.

"What the heck?" said Danny.

I couldn't figure out what it was, but there was a big magnet attached to a thumbtack, which was attached to a bent piece of cardboard which was connected to more thumbtacks and a wire that went straight up the side of the house and in through Randall's window. There was a little sign and an arrow beside the magnet.

Tree Rings, it said. *Pull the magnet.*

"Tree Rings?" said Danny.

"That's me," I told them and pulled the magnet away from the thumbtack. The piece of bent cardboard tipped over and the wire on the cardboard touched another thumbtack, which must have completed a circuit somewhere, because a few seconds later a voice from the speaker said, "Yo!" and we looked up. Randall was grinning at us from his window.

I picked up the mike under the bench. "How'd you know we were here?"

"Got a battery up here in my room, and a flashlight bulb. Bulb lit up when you pulled the magnet," Randall said through the speaker.

"No kidding!" said Danny, impressed.

"Come on down. We're going to put Paul's boat on the lake," I told him.

"*O-kay!*" Randall said, and in half a minute he burst out the door.

It was a nice morning, not as hot as it had been. Randall hadn't been down to Lake Tarragon yet, and I could tell that he liked walking through the tall grass, and then through the clump of trees at one end of the lake.

We let Randall have first go at it, and he guided the boat like he did this every day, grinning all the while.

"What we ought to do is each get a boat and put them all on the water at the same time," said Danny. "Have a navy. Get them to sail in formation and everything."

"That'd be great!" I said. I was glad Mickey wasn't along, just us four guys. We could have all kinds of fun like that down here. "Where'd you get yours, Paul? Do you think that Radio Shack would. . . ?"

We heard footsteps on the path behind us, and turned. There came Miss Quinn, leaning backwards to keep her balance in her high-heeled shoes, holding her skirt against her legs so it wouldn't catch on anything.

"Boys!"

We waited.

"I'm sorry to interfere again, but I tried to signal you back up there, and you didn't see me. I know this looks like fun, but I'm afraid I can't let you play down here."

"Why not?" said Paul. "What's the problem?"

"No boating," said Miss Quinn.

We couldn't believe it.

"This is a toy boat! We're not in the water. We're not even on the water!" Paul told her.

"I think it's up to me to interpret the rules, don't you? It's a question of liability."

"Miss Quinn, this isn't even as dangerous as fishing, and fishing is allowed," Danny argued.

She looked at us uncertainly. "I'm just going to have to check with Mr. Stacy on this. I'm sure that he had adults in mind when he said that fishing is permitted, and I feel quite certain he'd be upset if children were down here at all."

"But the rules don't say anything about children!" I said, sticking up for Paul and Danny. "I read them myself."

"Precisely. The lake is really for our aesthetic enjoyment, not recreation." (I gagged.) "And I'd feel a lot better if I checked this out with our general manager before I let anyone under eighteen down here."

"How long will that be?" Paul asked, the words coming out of his mouth fast and sharp, like bullets.

"Well, he oversees a number of developments, but he usually comes by every two weeks."

"We have to wait two weeks?" asked Danny. "Couldn't you call him and ask?"

Miss Quinn drew herself up until she was almost as tall as Paul. "Boys, when I hear from Mr. Stacy, I'll let you know. In the meantime, the lake is off-limits." She stepped aside and motioned toward the path, waiting. She was worse than my fourth-grade teacher.

For almost ten seconds, nobody moved. It was like we'd been zapped by a time machine and frozen into place. Randall, who hadn't said a word, stood there holding Paul's boat like it was glued to his hands. Suddenly Paul whirled and stormed up the path. The rest of us followed. I managed a semi-glare as I passed Miss Quinn, and at the top of the path, she went one way and we went another.

Randall gave the boat back to Paul, but Paul wouldn't even talk, and that's what bothered me.

"Stupid rules," I said, to get him started, but he didn't answer.

"Guess we better not buy any boats till we get word from the big cheese," said Randall.

"She could have called Stacy if she'd wanted. You can't tell me she can't get in touch with the general manager if she has to," said Danny.

"What's she got against kids anyway?" I added.

But Paul was ten feet ahead of us by now, not waiting for anyone, and when we reached Cajun Drive, we stopped and let him go.

"Dy-na-mite!" said Randall, shaking his head.

The Lookout

Two or three days went by. Paul and Danny talked on the phone a lot, but whenever Danny suggested doing something, Paul said no. We went over to shoot baskets, and he still looked like he'd had nails for breakfast, so I just stopped going. I mean, we were mad at Miss Quinn, too, but not that mad. He just couldn't let it go. Finally, I discovered one of the reasons he was so angry.

Just after they'd moved to Rosemary Acres, he told Danny, he found out he couldn't keep his cat. No pets allowed at Rosemary Acres, Miss Quinn had told him, except birds, hamsters, guinea pigs, and goldfish—anything in a bowl or cage, which figures. Mr. Bremmer hadn't read the contract carefully, and told Paul he couldn't afford to lose the down payment and find another place to live, so the cat would have to go. They gave it to a family in Aurora, fifteen miles away, but Paul could never forgive Miss Quinn. The business with the boat was the final straw.

For the first time, Danny himself seemed worried. At lunch on Sunday, Mom asked Danny a question and he didn't even answer.

"What's all this secrecy about?" she asked, and had to ask it again.

"What are you talking about?" Danny said.

"These phone calls back and forth between you and Paul. You always drag the extension phone into your room. What's up?" Mom looked directly at him.

Danny shoved back from the table. "Jeez! What is this, the Inquisition?" He stood and stomped upstairs.

Mom looked at me. "T.R., is there anything I should know?"

"I don't think so," I said, then wondered if I ought to tell her about the shoelaces, but I figured they were back at the store by now.

Mom toyed with her potato salad. "Mavis is a worrier, but she did have a point about you boys having to make all new friends if we moved here. I really don't know anything about the families of the friends you make, and I'm just going to have to trust that you guys will sort things out for yourselves."

I nodded.

"You'll keep an eye out, won't you?"

"Sure," I said, and my stomach flip-flopped. If I were a dog, I would have given a warning bark right then, but I didn't.

I went up to my room wondering exactly what was meant by "keeping an eye out." Just look out for Danny, I think she meant. She didn't say I had to tell her everything, so I was glad I hadn't promised her that. I was especially glad I hadn't promised her that when Danny got a call from Paul a short while later. As usual, he took the phone from the hallway and carried it into his room, then closed the door. And I knew what I had to do.

I'd been building a model of a tyrannosaur on my bed, but I got up in my stocking feet, crept out into the hall, and lay down outside Danny's door with my left ear up against the crack underneath. I took short little breaths through my mouth so that not even my breathing would give me away.

"That's dumb, Paul." It was the first thing I heard, then silence. Silence except for Danny's wiggling around. I never realized how much Danny fidgets when he's on the phone. He must have been sitting on one hip, then the other. Then he'd slap the phone cord, making it ripple. I could tell by the way it kept jerking on my side of the door.

"How are you going to get into her car?"

I lay like a dead man. Another long pause.

"How do you *know* the car will head for the lake? What if there's somebody down there?"

My heart was pounding like crazy.

"Yeah. . . ." Danny was saying. And then, "Yeah," again.

I couldn't believe what I was hearing. And I was hearing enough to know that Paul was planning to do something to Miss Quinn's car—release the emergency brake, probably—to send it rolling down the hill behind the office and straight for Lake Tarragon. Miss Quinn usually parked in the little gravel lot right behind the build-ing. All she had to do was go inside some day without locking her car, and Paul could put it in neutral. Even if she did lock it, Paul was mad enough that he would probably figure out a way to get in. I was glad it wasn't Randall's idea. Randall could have found a way not only to get in Miss Quinn's car, but to send it into the lake by remote control.

"Listen, I'll come over, okay?" Danny said, and when he came out of his room, I was lying on my bed again, building my dinosaur.

After Danny left, I got on my bike and rode over to Randall's. His dad came to the door holding a napkin, and I realized that they'd just come from church and were eating Sunday dinner.

"I'll wait out here," I told him.

"You like peach pie?" he said. "Come on in and have a piece." So I followed him into their dining room.

The whole family was dressed up, eating peach pie around the table.

"T.R.!" Leah cried, waving her spoon at me, and little drops of peach juice dropped down on the tablecloth.

Randall just grinned. "Bet you knew we were having pie."

"I only guessed," I said, thanking Mrs. Hayes when she put a slice in front of me, still warm from the oven, with ice cream melting on top. I didn't tell her that right then, pie was the last thing on my mind.

It was good, though, and I found myself running my finger over the saucer when I'd finished.

"We found a church down the highway that we like," Mrs. Hayes said. "Do you have a church here, T.R.?"

"Well, not exactly. We're thinking of becoming Unitarians," I told her.

"What kind of church is that?" asked Randall.

"Where you can't be excommunicated," I said knowingly.

"Oh," said Randall.

Mr. and Mrs. Hayes studied me curiously.

We went outside later, and sat facing each other on some trash cans out in the alley.

"I've got something to tell you, Randall, and you've got to promise you'll never tell another living soul," I said.

"How can I promise that until I've heard what it is?"

"You've just got to."

"Then you better not tell me."

"Listen, Randall, Paul's about to do something awful."

"So why are you telling me?"

"I want you to help me stop him."

"Man, you ever try to stop a freight train? Paul gets an idea in his head, *nothing's* going to stop him. What's he going to do, blow something up?" Randall asked.

"I don't know yet, but I think he's going to release the emergency brake on Miss Quinn's car and send it into the lake."

"Shoot! You tell Danny?"

"Danny already knows. He's over there right now, and what I'm afraid of is that he'll get mixed up in it, too."

"And if we go over there, *we're* in big trouble," said Randall. "Count me out."

"Please!" I said.

Randall shook his head. "You're just what my granddaddy warned me about."

"*Me?*"

"When he heard we were going to move near Chicago, he said I'd be running around with a street gang before you could count ten."

"I'm not trying to get you in trouble! I'm trying to keep Paul out of it!"

"If Paul's going to keep out of trouble, there isn't anybody that can do it but himself. That's what Dad always told me. If the brakes on Miss Quinn's car give out, I'm going to be as far away as I can get."

Aunt Mavis would have loved Randall, I knew. So would Aunt Cis and Grandma Flora. I sighed.

"Unitarians wouldn't even get excommunicated if they put a car in the lake?" Randall asked.

"I don't think so. What are you?"

"Methodist."

"Would they excommunicate you?"

"The pastor would turn me over his knee and paddle me hard, that's what."

Danny didn't come back all afternoon. I rode by Paul's house once or twice on my bike, but didn't see a trace of them.

That evening, though, Mom was down in the family room watching *60 Minutes*, and I had just taken a saucer of sugar wafers to my room when Danny came in.

"T.R.," he said, "Paul and I have a favor to ask you."

My heart stopped. "Yeah?"

"Listen." Danny's voice was husky. "Paul wants to make a statement. It's really important to him. But we won't tell you what he's going to do, so if anybody asks, you won't have to lie. You can honestly say you don't know."

My lips felt dry. "What do you mean?"

"He wants Rosemary Acres to know how he feels about all their lousy rules."

"So he's going to tell them?"

"In his own way."

I started to feel really sick. "So what am I supposed to do?"

"We want you to be a lookout."

"Danny, are you going to be doing this, too, whatever it is?"

"No, I'm the other lookout, at the other end of the block."

"Do you know what he's going to do?"

"Sort of. So, anyway, will you do it?"

"You're going to release the emergency brake on Miss Quinn's car so it crashes into the lake, aren't you?"

"Who told you that?" Danny stared at me hard. "You little creep! Were you listening in?"

"Danny, I'm worried about you. Mom's worried. I heard you talking when Paul called."

"We're not doing anything to her car," Danny said. "I

talked him out of it. But you know Paul, he's got to do something."

"W-when?"

"Tonight, late—after everyone's gone to bed."

"Is anyone going to get hurt, Danny?"

"No."

"Promise?"

"Yes."

My lips stuck together and I had to lick them before I could talk. "How are we going to get out of the house without Mom hearing? She always sleeps with her door open."

"We're going out your window and down the tree."

More than anything in the world right then, I wished we'd taken the townhouse over on Parsley Place.

"Danny," I said, "I'll do it, but please don't get into trouble."

"Don't worry."

I worried, all right. I stayed in my room all evening because I knew if I was around Mom, she'd know something was wrong. When her program was over, she washed another batch of clothes, sorted it, and finally poked her head in my room. "I'm all tuckered out. Going to bed. You guys get enough supper?"

"Yeah," I told her.

"Good. There are some bananas down there if anyone wants a snack. See you in the morning."

I turned out my own light about ten, and crawled under the sheets with my jeans on. I wanted to help Paul make a statement, but it really bothered me that they wouldn't tell me how. I had visions of Paul blowing up the Rosemary Acres office, and he and Danny being imprisoned for the rest of their lives. If Paul had something to say, why didn't he just write a letter? Why did he have to drag Danny into it?

I heard Danny go down the hall to the bathroom, the sound of the plastic cup thunking in the holder, and the flush of the toilet. I was sure I couldn't sleep, yet the next thing I knew, Danny was shaking my arm, saying, "Now," and my eyes popped open. He'd closed my door behind him.

We went over to the window. Danny opened it wide, and unlatched the screen, handing it to Paul, who was already waiting in the tree. Then, there I was, climbing out my window, Danny holding onto me until I had a good grip on the branch outside, and Paul had me by the other arm.

I was surprised we didn't make any more noise than we did. I'll bet professional burglars couldn't have been as quiet as we were. When we reached the ground, I saw an old gym bag sitting there on the grass. Dynamite, I thought.

Paul had one finger to his lips, and all the way down Basil Boulevard we kept to the shadows. We were heading toward Fennel Street, just as I suspected, and the Rosemary Acres office.

The office was at the end of a row of townhouses, with the door around the corner, facing the lake.

When we got as far as Dill Drive, one block short of Fennel, Paul whispered, "Okay, T.R., what I want you to do is stay on this corner. Keep out of sight. Stay in the bushes. But if you see any cars coming, or any people walking down Basil, I want you to whistle. You can whistle, can't you?"

"Yes . . ."

"That's all you have to do. You don't have to say anything, do anything, see anything—all you have to do is whistle if you see anybody on Basil."

"Where will Danny be?"

"Down one block on Fennel, watching in the other direction."

I squatted down in the bushes, and Paul and Danny took off. I thought how if I was a dog—a real dog, Lassie, for example—and I knew Danny was in trouble, I'd run after him, grab him by the belt, and pull him back. Instead, I just sat there in the bushes, letting him go.

One minute I was excited, the next minute scared. One minute I was the lookout, and then I'd think what Grandma Flora would say if she saw me here.

What if Danny went to jail? What if somebody thought he was a burglar and shot him? What would I tell Mom?

I kept waiting to hear an explosion or a police siren or something. I saw a car pull off Coriander and go up Basil in the other direction. A light came on in one of the townhouses, then went off again. No dogs barked because there weren't any dogs in Rosemary Acres—not anything warm and cuddly.

I wished I was back in Chicago right then, sitting on the porch with Aunt Cis, watching the lights go out in the houses across the street. "Watch," she always said. "See that window right over there? The light always goes off there first, then the one on the left, and then the one on the right."

I'd even settle for being in Milwaukee with Grandpa Gil. I closed my eyes tight and tried to will myself up to Milwaukee. But when I opened them again, I was right where I didn't want to be.

I don't know how long I was in the bushes. At some point I was so nervous I had to pee, but nobody saw. Another time I heard a faint whistle, and a little later a car came up the street from Fennel. I knew Danny had been warning Paul. The driver drove past me and went on toward Sage Circle.

At last, maybe a half hour later, I heard the bushes rustle, and then I saw Paul and Danny coming toward me in the shadows.

"Let's go," Paul whispered. And we hightailed it home.

It was harder getting up the tree than it was getting down, but somehow we made it inside. I expected to find Mom sitting on the bed, furious. Or maybe she'd be on the phone, crying her eyes out, calling the police to report us missing or kidnapped.

Nobody. No lights. No noise. Danny crawled in after me, then Paul handed him the screen and disappeared.

"He did it!" Danny whispered to me, after he'd latched the screen.

"What did he do?"

"I can't tell you, but it's done. It's what he wanted to do. Wait till tomorrow!"

"Just tell me one thing, Danny. Was it illegal?"

"Yes."

"Could he get in serious trouble?"

"If anyone finds out who did it, he could."

"Could you get in trouble?"

"If Paul does." He started toward my door. "I've got to get in bed before Mom wakes up."

"Danny!"

He turned.

"If two brothers go to jail, do they get to stay in the same cell?"

"Don't worry," Danny said again, and went across the hall.

This was only the start of things, I knew. Whatever Paul had done, he'd do more, and Danny would go with him, and before you knew it, their pictures would be in the newspaper and Mom would say, "He used to be a thoughtful, loving son until we moved to Rosemary Acres."

I took off my clothes, put on my pajama bottoms, and turned on my lamp. Then I took my old science notebook out of a drawer, got a pencil, and turned to a blank page at the back:

Dear Dad,

Things are really bad here at Rosemary Acres. Mom doesn't know, but Danny is probably in big trouble and we can't tell anyone. If he goes to jail, can you get him out?

Love, T.R.

P.S. Thanks for the balloons.

Bending the Rules

I was surprised I was still there the next morning. The sun was shining and music was floating up from downstairs. But I wouldn't let that fool me. I had to get outside and see if there were police around.

My letter to Dad was all ready except for a stamp. The address was easy because it was the University of California at Berkeley, and all you really had to remember was the zip code. I pulled on my shorts and T-shirt, went downstairs for a stamp, and managed to get out the front door without Mom seeing. I headed for the mail box at the corner of Cajun and Basil. I looked down Basil in the direction of Fennel Street, but I couldn't see anything. I mailed the letter and went back home.

"Danny still in bed?" I asked Mom. She was sitting at the table in her pajamas, reading the paper.

"Must be. Haven't heard a peep." She put down the paper, stretched, and smiled at me. "I'm *so* glad I took the whole summer off. I almost let them talk me into teaching three weeks of summer school, but I decided that might be too much. Now we're practically settled in, and I've still got a few weeks left. It's heaven."

I gave her a little smile and reached for the Captain Crunch. I wondered if it was safe to have breakfast with her, if my face would give me away. I unfolded the comics and tried to concentrate on how Spider-Man was going to get out of a trap the police had set for him. I looked at him climbing down a wall. Then I thought of Danny and Paul and me climbing down the tree. Was this the way juvenile delinquency began?

"Are you reading or are you daydreaming?" asked Mom, and I realized she wasn't looking at the newspaper anymore, she was looking at me. I knew I should have taken my cereal out on the back steps.

"I was wondering if twelve is a big stage in a guy's life," I said, trying to wing it. "If he changes a lot and everything."

"I think every year is a big stage in a person's life," said Mom. "But if you're noticing changes in Danny, it's probably the beginning of adolescence."

Somehow that made it sound like a disease.

"Does that make him do things he wouldn't have done before?"

"That he wasn't ready for before, maybe. Like wanting to be around girls. Is that what we're talking about here?"

I was glad I was turning the conversation away from what was bothering me most. "That and other stuff," I said.

"It's just a normal part of his growing up—girls," said Mom.

Danny appeared in the doorway. He still had a pillow crease on one cheek. "What are you talking about?" he asked, looking suspiciously at me.

"Sex," I told him, and passed him the cereal.

For the next hour, we didn't stick our heads outside, Danny and I. Nobody called. Nobody came. Danny still wouldn't tell me what Paul had done, so that if the police came, I wouldn't have to lie.

Mom was writing checks and listening to Beethoven's Pastoral Symphony at the same time. She told me if I listened hard, I could imagine peasants having a picnic in the meadow, then running for shelter during a thunderstorm. I was listening for thunder, all right. Every time I heard a noise outside, I went to the window.

"T.R.," Mom called a few minutes later. "Would you run this mortgage payment down to the office? I don't see why I should waste a stamp when it's only going a few blocks."

"All right," I said. I took the envelope, exchanged looks with Danny, and went outside to get my bike. I was Kit Carson, riding out to scout the territory. I rode down Cajun to the corner and turned left onto Basil.

The thing about Rosemary Acres is it looks like Rosemary had just swept and scrubbed everything in sight: the streets, the sidewalks—not a leaf out of place, not a scrap of paper, a wad of gum, a bottle cap. The landscape, as far as I could see, was the blue and gray of townhouses, the green and white of grass and sidewalks.

I rounded the curve on Basil Boulevard and passed the row of townhouses, heading for the one on the end. And then I skidded to a stop, because there in front of the Rosemary Acres office was a squad car. Standing out on the sidewalk were two policemen. And there, between the front windows of the office, with their regulation blue shutters, was a stoplight red door.

Ka-boom, ka-boom. That was my heart. One of the policemen stooped down to examine a speck on the sidewalk, but the other one had seen me coming.

"Hello?" he said.

I got off my bike and leaned it against a fire hydrant, then wondered if that was illegal and laid it on the grass.

"The door!" I said, still staring.

"Yeah, that's what we're here about," the other officer said. The men had been smiling before the saw me, but now they put on their official policemen expressions.

"Someone decided to do a little unauthorized redecorating," the first office said. "Would you happen to know who did it?"

I was really glad he asked it that way, not, "Would you have any idea who did it?" Because I didn't know for sure, I only suspected.

"No," I said.

"You're sure, now?"

I nodded. "When did it happen?"

"Last night. The manager says it was gray when she

left yesterday, and red when she got here this morning. The paint's dry, so I'd suspect someone came by a little after midnight."

"Well, I went to bed at ten," I told them. And then, "I've got to take this inside." I waved Mom's check.

Just as I reached the door, it opened and Miss Quinn came out. She looked at me hard, took the check, then turned to one of the policemen. "I just reached Mr. Stacy, and he'll be here this afternoon. He said we should go ahead and file a report, and if you get any information, please call him." She looked at me again.

"It's from Mom," I said, pointing to the envelope. "Our mortgage payment."

"Weren't you one of the boys who was down at the lake the other day?" she asked.

"What day?"

"The day some boys wanted to sail a boat?"

"We're not supposed to go to the lake," I said, repeating her orders. *Ka-boom, ka-boom, ka-boom.*

She turned to the officers again. "It could be one of those boys."

The officer looked at me, then at the door. "It's a pretty professional job for a kid, wouldn't you say? It was obviously done by someone experienced with a paintbrush. Kids usually throw paint, not brush it on. This isn't your ordinary case of vandalism."

I swallowed. The officer was walking across the grass and on around the building now, Miss Quinn and the other policeman following. I jumped on my bike and went barreling up Basil Boulevard. Inside our house, I tore up the stairs and into Danny's room, closing the door behind me.

Danny was on the bed eating grapes and looking through some baseball cards. "What happened?"

"The police are there!" I panted. "Paul painted the door red, didn't he? Miss Quinn says she thinks it was one of the boys down by the lake that day!"

Danny paused with a whole grape trapped between his lips, his eyes wide. He looked like a fish. Then he leapt off the bed and stood in the middle of his floor, looking scared. And when *Danny's* scared, I'm petrified.

We went to the top of the stairs. Beethoven's Pastoral Symphony had been replaced by his Victory Symphony. I recognized this one because it starts out, *Dot-dot-dot-dash . . . Dot-dot-dot-dash. . . .* Danny picked up the extension phone in the hall and dialed Paul's number. It rang and rang, but nobody answered. I figured Paul had left the country.

As soon as Danny hung up, though, the phone rang. This time I answered. It was Aunt Mavis. Danny went in his bedroom again and shut the door.

"How are you, T.R.?" I could tell she was choosing her words carefully. "How are things at Rosemary Acres?"

"Awful," I said, ready to tell anyone who would listen. "There are police all over the place."

"Uh huh," said Aunt Mavis. "That's nice. Go get your mother, would you?"

I called down to Mom, and when she took the call, I hung up and went back to Danny's room.

The worst thing is when there's nothing you can do.

Danny kept eating grapes like they were popcorn. I don't think he even knew what he was doing. He just kept popping them in his mouth, hardly chewing.

"Easy, Danny, you'll get the runs," I told him.

He ate another and another. Fifteen minutes went by.

The doorbell rang. We jumped like we'd been shot. We heard Mom's footsteps in the hall, the thunk of the door as it opened. Beethoven boomed from below. Then: "Danny? Someone wants to talk to you."

I swallowed. "If they take you to the police station, I'm coming with you."

"They won't let you," he said, slowly getting to his feet.

I followed him out in the hall. "Remember," I whispered, "they have to let you make one phone call."

He went down the stairs like a robot, and I was right behind him. There in the doorway stood Mickey.

"Mickey!" Danny sat down on the bottom step as though his knees had suddenly given out.

Mom poked her head in from the living room, and I realized they'd never been introduced. "Mickey, Mom," I said.

"Hi, Mickey," Mother said, and went on out to the kitchen.

Mickey stared at Danny. "You okay? I thought we could all ride around or something."

"Let's go," I said, pulling Danny to his feet. "We're going out riding, Mom," I called.

When we got outside, Mickey said, "What's the matter with you two?"

"We've got to talk," Danny said. "Someplace private."

Mickey studied us. "Follow me," she said.

We went up Basil Boulevard in the other direction, past Paul's street, past the playground at Sage Circle, on beyond Pepper Road to where Basil curved and crossed Ginger Avenue, then ended in a field.

"It's over on Hillman's property," Mickey said, "but we can get through the fence. Come on."

We put down our bikes and held the barbed wire apart for each other as we climbed through. There was a narrow path along the fence and we followed it until we came to a tiny six-plot cemetery, right out in the middle of nowhere, surrounded by a low iron fence. All but one of the names on the tombstones was Hillman. What was really eerie, though, was that there was a big mulberry tree overhanging the plot, and mulberries had dropped down on some of the tombstones, leaving streaks of red that looked like blood.

Mickey sat down on the tombstone of Rose Hillman Blaine, but I wasn't sure if you could do that—if it's one of the Ten Commandments or not. But I figured Mickey was probably more religious than we are, and if she sat on a grave, it must be okay. So I sat down on "Fred J. Hillman, Father."

"Now. What's happened?" Mickey asked, and Danny told her everything.

"Bright red?" asked Mickey.

"Stoplight red," I told her. A mulberry fell in my lap, and I ate it.

Danny talked on about how ticked off Paul was about

all the rules here at Rosemary Acres, how he had to give away his cat, how Miss Quinn seemed to have it in for us, whatever we did.

He told Mickey that Paul had been determined to release the brakes on Miss Quinn's car and send it into the lake, but that he'd talked him out of it—out of that and into something else: painting the door.

I knew that was just the way Danny would handle it, too. If he stopped Paul completely, the anger would go on. If he let him go ahead and wreck Miss Quinn's car, he would be in big, big trouble. So now they were only in medium-sized trouble: six months in jail, maybe, instead of a year.

It was cool and shady beneath the mulberry tree, and I didn't want to leave, not ever. Danny said we'd better stay for a while, so we waited for mulberries to drop, and tried to figure out whether painting a door was a felony or a misdemeanor. I couldn't figure out how we were supposed to know when it was time to go back—when the police started across the field with bloodhounds, maybe.

Suddenly Danny sat up straight. "What if the police go around to the houses of all the boys who were down at the lake that day, T.R.? That means they'll come to ours, and Mom will freak out. We've got to get home."

But then I thought of Randall, who didn't know anything at all about the door. I had to warn him. "Let's stop off at Randall's first," I said. "He's got to know, too."

We got on our bikes and this time rode down Ginger instead of Basil, so we could stop at Parsley Place. While

Mickey and Danny waited out by the curb, I went to the front door and knocked. Randall came, but he wasn't smiling.

"I can't," he said, when we asked him to come out.

"Later?"

"Probably not ever."

Ka-boom, ka-boom. "Why not?"

And then Mrs. Hayes came to the door, Leah beside her. "Because someone around here got in a heap of trouble and it looks like they're trying to blame Randall, that's why," she said. "I don't know who it was painted that door, but I don't like it that the police came here. And until we know who did it, Randall's not going anywhere with anyone." She didn't sound like a secretary or a teacher, either one. She sounded like the superintendent of public schools.

"The police were already here?" I said in a squeaky voice. Leah pressed her nose against the screen and studied me seriously.

Randall nodded. "And you all were next on their list."

I didn't even think to tell Mrs. Hayes that I knew who painted that door. I just jumped on my bike again and we took off for Paul's. He'd gotten us into this and it was up to him to get us out. We told Mickey to go on home—we didn't want any more people mixed up in this than there were already—but we were going to camp on Paul's steps till he came home.

Paul was just going into his house when we rode up.

"Where have you been?" Danny asked. It was the first time he sounded angry at Paul.

"Went shopping with Dad. He stayed at the mall to get his glasses changed, so I walked on home." He looked hard at Danny. "What's happening?"

"The police have been to Randall's."

"Shit!" Paul looked at me.

"He knows," said Danny.

I told Paul what had gone on at the office, and then what Mrs. Hayes had said. "She says Randall can't go out with us anymore until they find out who painted that door," I added.

Paul didn't move for a moment, and I knew this wasn't what he had planned—that somebody else was going to get in trouble. I guess when you make a statement, you figure they'll either find out who did it or they won't, but you don't think about them blaming someone else. The police had probably come to Paul's house, too, but he wasn't home.

"Shit!" he said again, then whistled through his teeth, rubbing his head with one hand. "Wait here for me," he said at last, and went on inside.

When he came out a few minutes later, he was carrying a half-used bucket of gray paint and a brush. He slipped the bucket over the handlebars of his bike, and Danny and I followed him to the Rosemary Acres office.

The police cruiser was gone. There was a Lincoln Continental there instead—a white Lincoln with white leather upholstery. We walked single file through the door, and came face-to-face with Miss Quinn and a man we didn't know.

"Boys?" said Miss Quinn in her ice-cube voice.

Miss Quinn stared. "Them!" she said to the man in the blue blazer and tan slacks.

He was a little on the heavy side and had thick gray hair. He studied Paul quizzically, then stared at the paint bucket. "Are you the one who painted our door?" he asked.

"Sir!" said Paul loudly, clicking his heels together again. His dad must have taught him to do that.

"I was right, Mr. Stacy!" said Miss Quinn.

Mr. Stacy came around and sat on the front of Miss Quinn's desk. He looked more puzzled than angry. "I guess the obvious question is why."

"To make a statement, sir!" said Paul, still with one hand to his forehead. When Paul dishes out the sarcasm, he gives you a big helping.

"At ease, soldier. A statement about what?"

"About the rules," said Paul. "Rules for no good reason."

"And when we asked Miss Quinn to call you, she wouldn't," added Danny.

Miss Quinn looked flustered. "It wasn't that . . . I didn't. . . ."

"Any rule in particular?" Mr. Stacy interrupted her.

"No model boats on the lake," I told him, wanting to be a part of the protest.

"Ah," Mr. Stacy nodded. "Well, the lake *is* cause for concern. Residents like it, but we're always worried about children."

"I tried to tell them about liability," said Miss Quinn.

"We don't want to put a fence around it because that

detracts from its appeal, but at the same time, we don't want to encourage children to go down there," Mr. Stacy said. "However, if we don't specifically forbid children to go to the lake, then I don't see how we can object to their sailing something on it, as long as they don't go in the water."

Miss Quinn was thinking that over.

"Therefore," said Mr. Stacy, "if you repaint my door, which I see you are prepared to do, you may sail your boats on the lake."

We all grinned at each other. We even grinned at Miss Quinn, but she didn't return the favor.

"And I want a professional-looking job on that door," Mr. Stacy added, following us outside. "I don't think that paint you brought quite matches. We'll go over to maintenance and get some."

I wanted to ask something while I had the chance. "Was it you who thought up cow-pattie bingo?" I was sure that an idea like that could not possibly have come from Miss Quinn.

Mr. Stacy laughed. "I'm an old farm boy from way back. I figured it might be a lot of fun."

We had to explain everything to Mom, because she was waiting with fire in her eyes when we got home. Like Danny said, the police had been by, and she freaked out.

"This is the last thing I expected to happen out here in the country," she said. I waited for her to tell Danny, "You were always a thoughtful and loving son until we moved to Rosemary Acres," but she didn't.

"It's over, Mom," Danny told her. "The door's repainted and Paul did a good job."

"It's not the door, Danny. It's the way Paul went about things."

"He probably couldn't think of anything better."

"And neither could you?"

Danny was sitting with his feet propped against the edge of the coffee table. He was examining a hole in his jeans. "Mom, you don't know the half of it," he said at last. "If you knew what Paul could have done . . . . It was important to get his feelings out."

"And maybe Danny Scarlino's, too?" Mom said quietly.

I realized something then: Paul was Danny's safety valve. *Danny* had to cut loose sometimes, and he did it through Paul.

"Once in a while, maybe," Danny said. "But everything's fine now, Mom. Really."

But the fact was, everything wasn't. We still didn't see much of Randall. His dad let him talk to us if we met at the pool or something, but when I went around to his patio to talk to him over the mike, the mike and speaker set were gone. Whenever we stopped by his house and asked him out, he had to make an excuse. I felt really bad, but Randall felt even worse.

"Just can't reason with them, man!" he whispered to me once through the screen.

Maybe life's like that. You solve one problem and another pops up. We had the lake, though, and about every day that next week we carried Paul's boat down there and took turns guiding it around on the water. Randall would have loved it.

And then, one afternoon when Mom was out, Danny and I were just coming back from the lake when we saw a strange car in front of our townhouse, but it was empty. We looked toward the door, and there on the front steps was Dad.

Pioneers

It's really weird when you haven't seen your dad for two years and he shows up on your doorstep. He looked a little different than I remembered him. The hair above his ears was gray, and his jaws seemed fatter or something. Otherwise, I guess he looked the same.

At first Danny and I just stared, then we got off our bikes, and you know what I said? After not seeing my father for two years, the first thing out of my mouth was, "What happened to the car with the hood ornament?"

Dad laughed. "I traded the Plymouth in, T.R., but not for this. This is just a car I rented at the airport. How are you guys? Gosh, Danny, you're so much bigger. You're both bigger!"

"We didn't know you were coming, Dad. Does Mom know you're here?" Danny asked.

"Nobody knows but Cis, and I just called her this morning. I was beginning to wonder if you'd all gone off on a trip or something. I assumed, from T.R.'s letter, that you'd be here, though."

"What letter?" asked Danny, looking at me.

I just stared down at the sidewalk.

"A letter telling me that you're in big trouble, Danny, and wanting to know if I could put up bail."

I wished Dad hadn't told that. I could feel my face getting hot. "I was worried about you, Danny," I mumbled.

"Well, I was pretty worried when I got the letter," Dad went on. "And since you said your mother didn't know anything about it, I figured I'd better come out here and see for myself. Where is she?"

"At the beauty parlor," I said.

Dad stood up. "So this is where you live, huh? Looks nice."

"Want to see inside?" I asked, and he said yes, so we gave him a tour. When we got to my room, I showed him the window we climbed out of, and the tree, and then Danny told him the whole story of what happened.

"So that's all there is to it?" asked Dad.

"That's it," said Danny.

I couldn't tell if Dad was relieved or angry. Angry that he'd flown all the way out here for nothing, maybe, but glad it wasn't worse than it was.

"Sounds to me like this Paul character handled it pretty well, once he did what he did." Dad waited. We waited. "Well, listen!" he said finally, slapping a hand on each of our shoulders. "Let's go out for ice cream. Any good ice-cream places around?"

We told him about the one at the mall. Danny left a note for Mom, and then we climbed in Dad's rented car and took off down the highway.

But it wasn't the same. The Toyota didn't smell anything like the car I remember. This one smelled of new leather and other people's cigarettes. Danny sat up front with Dad, while I sat in the backseat and tried to think of interesting things to talk about.

How's your graduate assistant, Dad? Nope, not that.

Do you miss Mom? Not that either.

How's California? That was okay.

Do you ever miss Danny and me? I didn't think I wanted to ask him that, so he wouldn't have to lie.

The waitress brought hot-fudge sundaes for Danny and me, mocha-caramel for Dad. We talked about Rosemary Acres and Grandma Flora's visit. About the fireworks on the Fourth of July, and cow-pattie bingo. And I realized suddenly that we were talking about memories. We'd only been here five weeks or so, and already we had something to go in the memory bank, as Aunt Cis puts it.

It would have been better if the ice-cream parlor wasn't so noisy. Sometimes when Dad asked a question, he had to lean across the table to hear our answers.

"You know, T.R., maybe it's a good thing you wrote, because it made me do what I should have done long ago: get on a plane and come out to see you guys."

"Why didn't you?" I asked.

"I'm not sure. For the first year, of course, I was in Greece. Then it seemed awkward, after a whole year, to suddenly show up, and—now I'm not blaming you,

Danny—but when you didn't answer my letter, I figured you didn't want to see me. So one year became two."

"It wasn't that we didn't want to see you, Dad. I just didn't get around to answering your letter, that's all."

"You could have called," said Dad.

"So could you," said Danny.

Dad turned his water glass around and around on the table. "You're right. The truth of the matter is, I'm not much good at being a father—being married. People are good and not so good at different things, you know. . . ."

Part of me wanted to say, "You rat!" and part of me was glad he wasn't feeding us a lot of bullshit. That's one thing I can't stand: bullshit.

"I regret that I wasn't a better husband and father," Dad went on, "but one thing I've never regretted is that you boys were born. You're fine guys, and I'm mighty proud of you. Really. I know I'm missing out on a lot by not being around while you're growing up, but if you ever need me for the big things, I'll be there."

Danny had stopped eating, and was toying with his spoon. I could see the way the corners of his mouth tugged down. I think Danny missed Dad more than I did, because he'd known him longer and had more memories. It wasn't the big things we needed Dad for so much as the little things, I was thinking. When something big happens, a lot of people step in to help. It's all the small stuff you have to handle alone that hurts.

I guess Dad realized how Danny was feeling, because he said suddenly, "Well! Let's get you guys back to Rose-mary Acres before your mom thinks you've been kidnapped. I'm staying at Celia's tonight, and I'll head back to Berkeley in the morning."

Danny made a quick swipe of his eyes and went on twirling the spoon while Dad took out his American Express card and paid for the ice cream.

And then we were driving back down the highway toward the blue and gray and green and white of Rosemary Acres. When he stopped in front of the house, Dad said, "Let's not wait so long next time, okay? You can call me collect anytime, Danny. You too, T.R. And I'm going to be better at communicating myself."

He leaned over and hugged Danny, then twisted around in the seat and hugged me.

Danny tried to make a joke. "You know that book, Dad, *From Boyhood to Manhood*?"

Dad stared. "You mean that thing's still around? That book Mom gave me when I was young?"

Danny nodded. "Well, we've got it now. And it stinks."

We all laughed then, and that helped, but only for a while. Because one minute Danny and I were standing out on the sidewalk waving good-bye, and the next Danny was going in his room, closing the door, and I was lying face down on my bed, gulping and gulping, trying not to cry. But I did anyway. Mom wasn't home yet and I was glad. I had to get this out.

Why did I miss Dad if he was such a louse, I wondered. But it was a dumb question, because he hadn't been a louse 100 percent of the time; we'd done some nice things together. And he was the only dad I had, after all.

After a while I felt something bump my leg, and

turned to see Danny sitting on the bed beside me, his eyes red. I sat up on one elbow and just let the angry tears come. "Why couldn't he be good at marriage and bad at teaching, Danny? Or bad at fixing a car and good at being a dad?"

"I don't know, T.R. But it's going to be okay," he said. Danny was trying to be Man of the House again. "Let's got out and find Paul—go ride around or something."

I nodded. When our eyes looked okay, we went to get Paul. Then we went down to Coriander to pick up Mickey, and of course Norman had to come, too, in a pink T-shirt with a panda on the front.

"Where'll we go?" Danny asked.

"We could show Paul our secret place," said Mickey, which of course didn't make it secret anymore, but that was okay. We headed up Ginger Avenue.

Mickey and Danny were up ahead, Paul behind them, and I was just passing Parsley Place when I glanced up the road and saw Mrs. Hayes running down it.

"Wait a minute," I called to the others, and pulled over to the curb.

"Leah!" Mrs. Hayes was yelling. "Leah!"

"Hey guys!" I called to the others. Norman had pulled up behind me. Danny, Mickey, and Paul circled around and rode back.

I turned my bike up Parsley. "What's wrong?" I called.

"We can't find Leah! She was playing in the yard the last I saw her." Mrs. Hayes looked desperate.

"We'll help look," Danny said.

"Roy's not home, and I just put Leah outside with a

bucket of water and some cups to play with and. . . ."

Randall came running up the road. "I checked next door, Mom. They haven't seen her," he panted.

"Why don't we fan out," said Paul. "Everybody take a different section so we don't keep looking in the same place."

Danny and Paul headed for the alley behind the Hayes's townhouse, Mickey and Randall went back up Parsley Place in the direction we'd come, and Norman and I started looking around the backs and sides of the other townhouses.

I wondered if we weren't all thinking the same thing: the lake. Was it possible she could have got over there somehow? She would have had to cross the whole development, though, and somehow that just didn't seem likely. But I had a little taste of what Mr. Stacy and Miss Quinn felt about kids—small kids, anyway—being down there.

We must have searched for ten minutes, everybody calling Leah, looking under porch furniture on other people's patios, behind steps and bushes. Mrs. Hayes had tears in her eyes when I went back to the street where she was standing.

"I'm going to call Roy and tell him to come home," she said, going inside the house.

I was pretty good at figuring out what it felt like to be a dog, I thought, and wondered if I could feel what it was like to be a little kid. If I was three years old, and only about three feet high, where would I go? What would I see outside that would catch my eye?

I figured that little kids don't take in the whole world when they're outdoors. They stop to step in puddles, pick up leaves, touch a worm, poke a bug. So I looked around at the ground. What I saw up ahead were daisies—some kind of wildflower, anyway, bright yellow—growing along the road where the townhouses stopped and the sidewalk gave way to weeds. If I was three feet tall, I'd see those yellow flowers, I thought.

I headed down Parsley Place in the other direction, and followed it around the bend. There was a wilted daisy—just the yellow part—lying in the road like a button. Then another. My pulse picked up. Someone had come along picking flowers, but only the yellow part. Ten feet ahead there was still another on the road. I looked all around.

"Leah!" I yelled. "Hey, Leah!"

And then I heard someone cry. It was so faint it could have been a bird, though. I listened again. It came again, and it seemed to be coming from on down the road. I ran.

There was a drainage ditch along one side, and a pipe that ran under the road. I crouched down, my head in the weeds, and looked in the pipe. Something moved.

"Leah?" I called.

I heard a sob.

I leapt up, and ran back to the curve in the road. "She's here!" I yelled to the others, and everyone came running.

We all got down in the ditch. Mrs. Hayes was calling instructions. "Just crawl out here to me, honey," she said, but Randall's little sister only cried harder. From what I could see, her leg was twisted around and I figured she was either caught on something, or she couldn't get her leg straightened out again. I tried to wriggle into one end of the pipe, but my shoulders wouldn't go through.

"Want me to call the fire department, Mom?" Randall kept asking.

"Let me try," said Norman.

While the rest of us watched, Norm the Nerd, in his red shorts and pink T-shirt, got down on his stomach, put his arms into the pipe, then his head, and began inching his way inside. His head, one shoulder, the other shoulder . . .

"If I get stuck, you guys . . ." he called shakily.

"We'll pull you out, Norm," I promised. "You're doing fine. Keep going."

Leah's crying died down to a whimper when she realized there was someone else in the pipe with her.

"I've got her," Norm called at last, and we all cheered as his feet came out, then his legs, his butt, his shoulders, and finally Leah, tear-streaked and dirty. Mrs. Hayes hugged her close, and untangled her shoe buckle from a branch that had been wedged with her inside the pipe.

"Nice going, Norm," I said. He beamed. Like Dad says, everyone is good at some things, not so good at others.

"Nuts!" Randall joked. "I wanted to call the fire department."

We figured we'd better leave, but Mrs. Hayes said,

"You come right home and have something to eat, now—every last one of you."

I don't think I ever turned down something to eat in my life, unless it was when I had the flu. We trooped up the road to the alley, and then to the Hayes's patio. Leah sat in Randall's lap as we drank lemonade and feasted on chocolate-chunk cookies.

It was pure luck that we were riding by when we did. If we hadn't helped find Leah, though, I think we would have thought of another way to make it up to the Hayeses. They couldn't stay mad forever, but this couldn't have happened at a better time.

Mickey was telling us how she got separated once from her mother in a department store, and Paul remembered getting lost when he was seven. Danny told them about the time I crawled under my bed and went to sleep, and the whole neighborhood was out searching for me.

"Hey, Toll Road," Randall said. "You know what we could do? Fix Leah up with some kind of radio transmitter on a collar, so that no matter where she went, we could track her."

"You want real trouble, you try putting a dog collar on your sister," Mrs. Hayes told Randall, and we laughed.

It was just about then I realized we'd been through a couple of things together now, our gang from Rosemary Acres. I guess it's stuff like this you remember, and the memories that make you friends.

In fact, my fourth-grade teacher would probably say we were pioneers, like the ones who went west in covered wagons, each having to depend on the other. It was uncharted territory in the land of blue and gray, and if that was scary—well, we still wanted to stick around and see what happened next.